DAREDEVIL SEX

Greta wasn't like many of the girls Nick had known. She was as mature as she was beautiful, as ingenious as she was stacked. She caressed him, fondled him, whispered to him, half-undressed him—she was hungry as hell for a man and she came on strong.

Nick relaxed, shivered as she applied a special combination of touches. Why should he fight it? It was sheer heaven—and it was all in the line of duty.

Of course when she found out who he really was, he'd be dead . . .

> *Killmaster mixes pleasure and business in lethal doses—and uncovers a macabre espionage plot that's too terrifyingly perfect to fail*

THE NICK CARTER/KILLMASTER SERIES

NICK CARTER

A Killmaster Spy Chiller

THE HUMAN TIME BOMB

AWARD BOOKS
NEW YORK

TANDEM BOOKS
LONDON

Second Award printing 1970

Dedicated to

The Men of the Secret Services

of the

United States of America

AWARD BOOKS are published by:
Universal Publishing & Distributing Corporation
235 East Forty-fifth Street, New York, N. Y. 10017

TANDEM BOOKS are published by:
Universal-Tandem Publishing Co. Ltd.,
14 Gloucester Road, London, SW7, England

Manufactured in the United States of America

...ter the warning slip had been in place *eight hours,*
...d Santos was notified in Control. He made cautious
...to Denver. Because the yellow tag was there the next
...ing, he notified David Hawk, in accordance with procedure.

AXE has a tight, direct chain of command. As the respected head, David Hawk can obtain appropriations from
Congress as easily as the seventeen other major intelligence-
security units. But perhaps it is part of the secret of AXE's
efficiency that it operates on a budget only a fraction of that
of the other agencies.

You can get involved in just spending money and keeping
it coming. Administration smothers action. On the other
hand, AXE has a limited number of men in reserve. There's
no featherbedding.

It's interesting to note that while FBI men are "agents" and
many people refer to the "CIA boys," AXEmen are often referred to by insiders as "representatives." Senators in the
know and many in Executive and in Justice use the term.

AXEmen—and David Hawk—appreciate this, although
oddly they refer to themselves as AXEmen and by their code
letters and numbers.

Hubie Dumont entered the N category because of his intelligence and athletic qualifications. If he had lived and proved
his ability and judgment he might have become a Killmaster.
These few AXEmen are representatives of the United States
with the right of unquestioned action in emergencies. An able
but free-styling columnist who once discovered some details
of an AXE case labeled them Killmasters. AXEmen don't
care for the name but it stuck.

Hubie Dumont might have made it (only one out of fifteen
does, on the final exams and tests, and remember, they're already seasoned AXEmen)—but when David Hawk received
the "failed to report" slip he gave no thought to that. From
his downtown Washington office near DuPont Circle he
talked with Santos on the private, scrambled circuit.

"Bernie, about N82—any other news from out there?"

"None, sir. Teletypes are clean. State BCI there has nothing. Sheriff's office also blank. There's a town force that
doesn't get that way very often. Just a three-man force. I

haven't called them because there might be complication. They have a C-4 rate. Shall I try 'em?"

Hawk's seamed features were very grave. "No. What position on N3?"

"Paris. Return tomorrow."

"Please route him to me. Quickest."

"Yes, sir."

Hawk hung up and lifted a file from the lower drawer of his desk. It was marked REED-FARBEN LTD. He scanned the few sheets in it.

You could consider Reed-Farben just another quick-growth firm in the booming pharmaceutical field, or you could consider it damn mysterious. It could depend on your experience—and intuition. They were well financed, but some of it was foreign money. Their principals were never seen, but neither are many top executives. They employed German and Japanese and French scientists, but so do many companies. They built their own airstrip and turned down federal financing aid. They profitably produced industrial chemicals and medicines but they employed top biologists and one doctor who was an authority on heart and kidney transplants. Oddly enough, he hadn't given an interview since he went to work for Reed-Farben.

The muscles at the corners of Hawk's mouth tightened. Young N82 had been sent to have a look. When an AXEman failed to report—especially a determined young man like Hubie Dumont—you could be sure your original intuition had been reliable. Hawk closed the folder slowly and put it in his upper right drawer—the one he called his "urgent."

*   *   *

Martha Wagner missed Hubie. She was the only person in the world, outside of AXE, to notice the bare spot he left in society. She missed his company for the midnight snack. She looked for him in vain at morning coffee time and for lunch.

Martha was a young woman with purposeful go, plumpish where it looked good. She was pretty, with more than just nice looks.

She was the Martha of the neon sign near the road that

announced MARTHA'S DINER. HOME COOKING, COCK-
TAILS. Six years ago her father's lungs had quit, too early,
plugged with mine dust. but he left a $6000 policy plus bits
from the company. and the union.

When it happened Martha had been working for nearly
two years in Perlinson's Restaurant in Colorado Springs. She
dodged hands made good money and tried to keep her
brother Pete sober enough to stay with his latest reporter's
job on the *Rocky Mountain News*. On their rare holidays
they came up to Copperpot Valley to ski. and Martha took a
long look at Lucky Ed's Diner. Lucky was seventy, and the
diner was filthy but still did a nice gross. It was the only
game in town.

She bought it, kept Bob Half-Crow, one of Perlinson's best
cooks. and a few months later you had to wait for a seat in
Martha's Diner during the tourist rush.

Peter Wagner. good reporter or not, mixed gin with jour-
nalism in too strong a blend and became his sister's assistant
manager. It was an interesting situation, because Bob Half-
Crow hated booze- "It ruined my race." When not cooking
—and now he had four helpers—he made a marvelous head
bartender—friendly precise as a mixer and entertaining. He
once confided to Martha. "I love to serve white men alcohol.
I tell 'em, 'I think you had enough.' but they never listen."

He made a fine watchdog for Pete. They were close friends
except on the periodic occasions when Pete took one, then
two, and the rest could not be counted. Bob once went all the
way to Boise to bring him home.

Some years ago Martha had had Ed's wooden structure
bulldozed into splinters and built a new diner-restaurant-
lounge all stainless steel and Formica inside, varnished native
wood on the exterior During the tourist and ski seasons you
still often waited for a table.

Martha missed Hubie Dumont because he came across to
her the way she did to many people. He was alert, friendly,
and you could tell he was a hell of a lot more than he
seemed. And Martha was healthy, her vital juices churning
even though she worked ten hours a day and refused many
an offer. Cautiously, she knew that a man like Hubie, al-

though she had only talked with him five times, could be what she was looking for and needed.

He said he was a chemical salesman, "Just a peddler."

He had watched the operation and complimented her and drawn most of her life's story out of her. She thought he might ask her for a date—perhaps next time?

On the night he was carried, totally unconscious, into the big windowless building he had tried to investigate, Martha Wagner sat over a beer long after closing. Then she smiled her firm little smile, shrugged and drove the half mile along the highway to the cottage she shared with Pete.

*   *   *

Martha Wagner was surprised when another one showed up. It must be my year, she thought, or I'm getting eager. This one was bigger than Hubie, with brown hair instead of red, but he had the same easy way of getting acquainted. Polite and reserved, yet you felt he was interested in you and you were drawn to him. He was handsome. Some girls might not think so if they preferred the thin-cheeks-and-sideburns type. Jim Perry had a full round chin and a mouth above it that grinned easily though not often. She thought he had the keenest eyes she had ever seen, next to Bob Half-Crow's.

He drove a four-year-old Ford but it was clean and dent free. He said he came from Pittsburgh and points north and south—making that small grin—and needed a job. The steel mills were just too much.

Martha sized up Jim Perry carefully that first evening, staying long after the time she usually went home for her evening break after the dinner rush. She wasn't sure why—(I am not, she told herself frequently and again this evening, burning for a man). She was now twenty-seven, a hard worker and vibrantly healthy, smarter than many, and often had the company of her brother Pete in their immaculate little cottage. On Tuesday mornings she had nice talks with the once-a-week maid. She subscribed to four magazines and a New York paper. Pete was teaching her to play chess. Why should I be lonely for a man?

She decided she was sizing Jim Perry up through caution.

After all, there were the six slot machines in the foyer between the bar and the dining room, and of course she creamed the top of the gross from Internal Revenue like everyone else. This Jim Perry could be one. He was so clean and quiet. And wouldn't you say too intelligent for a steelworker and truck driver?

The truck-driving bit came up after he approached her in her "private" end booth with a question. He asked it with soft politeness and a shy grin, not the overconfident nearbluster of some of them. "Miss Wagner? My name's Jim Perry. Could you recommend a place to stay around here that's reasonable and clean? I'm not broke. Not holding heavy."

She gave him her check-cashing-and-credit appraisal. That was when she noticed the keen, wide-set gray eyes and the man-boy roundness of his chin and cheeks. He was no boy. About her own age. Noting the look, Nick Carter was glad he wasn't wearing contact lenses (the AXE makeup department gave you any color eyes; hair and style features you needed, but this girl searched for flaws).

"Try the Alpine. Four miles west, you won't miss it. Don't let the little old cottages fool you. Abe Phipps runs a clean, quiet place."

"Thanks." He hesitated shyly. "Would you cash a check for me? I don't mean now. You put it through and give me the money when it clears."

"Fair enough. Who's it on?"

"Monongahela Steel Fabricating." He gave her a pay check for $159.32. "My last week. I asked Bob at the bar and he said you might—"

"Sure." She hesitated an instant. Her private booth was respected by the regulars. If a newcomer sat down without an invitation, big Bob Half-Crow would arrive shortly with the suggestion, "why don't you sit in that one over there?" "Sit down, Jim," she said.

"Thanks. Can I buy?"

"A beer. On me. Don't start buying the conductor a ticket."

"I usually don't. But you being a lady, I broke my rule."

They laughed. Bob Half-Crow came over. Martha gave

him the O.K. signal—left palm flat on the table—and said, "Two beers, please, Bob."

Nick said, "You run a tight ship. I remember when this was Lucky Ed's. You were lucky to live if you ate a full meal."

"You've been up here before?"

"Came up skiing. When Lyman Electronics built the first building where Reed-Farben is now. I tried to get a job but they didn't have anything. I figured I'd like to live here. All the hunting and skiing I wanted. When I couldn't take any more steel cuttings in my face I headed back."

"You're going to try at Reed-Farben?"

"Thought I would."

"They're chemicals, not steel."

"I've got a Colorado truck driver's ticket. But I'll take anything."

"They want security clearance."

"Got it too. We did a lot of war stuff at Monongahela Steel."

Martha nodded thoughtfully. The check and the background talk removed her doubts. Jim Perry was a handsome rambling man, not a Revenue Agent or from the State BCI office; they were even worse—you had to lay low awhile if you got an eager beaver or pay if he was a black box man. She studied Jim as he relaxed and watched the crowd.

Three bartenders were busy, two up-and-down and one covering the rear handles and service bar. Bob Half-Crow stood easy, watching the kitchen, the roughnecks and the dampers. It was Pete's night off. Nick admired the setup. Working stiffs on this side, isolated from the tourist dining room across the foyer, with the kitchen feeding through double doors in between. You got the families, and the gross on this side must be good. Two small pool tables had waiting groups and the shuffleboard gang were betting ten dollars a side. This gang could get tough, but Bob Half-Crow, his black eyes everywhere and standing straight as an oak and as big across as Nick himself, was undoubtedly a quick cooler.

"How long have you had the place, Miss Wagner?" Nick asked.

"Five years. I tore down Ed's old place after the first two."

"I was up here about then. That would be just about the time Reed-Farben made their move." The gray eyes met hers, quizzical but warm. She felt a tiny shiver inside. Easy, Martha, she warned herself, a rambling truckdriver!

"That's right," she replied.

"So you picked the perfect time to make your move. Business was due to at least triple and you bought the only eatery. You're a smart businesswoman."

"Just lucky, maybe."

He chuckled and one of his brown eyebrows went up and down as if agreeing to something they both understood. She thought, sonuvagun, he's a smart one. Even Bob and Pete hadn't figured out that Pearly Abbott, ex-congressman and wheeler-dealer in everything from banks to real estate in eight states, had given her the tip at Perlinson's—of which he had a piece.

Later he had said, "Martha, I never thought you'd move so fast. And did you have to steal our best cook?"

She had told him Perlinson's had several, but she only had Bob for a gamble that was make or break for her. Abbot's three chins had bounced affectionately at her above his spotless white forty-dollar shirt and she let him get his feel. She could have eluded his plump hand, hidden by the tablecloth, but when you owed—

A year later she didn't have to favor Pearly or anybody, although you never crossed Pearly. He came in at least once a month, sometimes with a party, which cost her an unpaid check of about $100, unless he gave her a hint that someone with him would pay. It hadn't taken her long to figure out that he had more than a casual interest in Reed-Farben Ltd.

"Jim," she said, "Reed-Farben hires a lot of people, but they're sticky. I mean there are local boys they won't touch, yet lots of people drive a hundred miles a day to work there. The personnel man is Kenny Abbott. He's—connected politically. You won't get to see him right away, I don't suppose, but if you do—you can say I gave you his name. Tell him—I cash your checks."

Martha's eyes, a dark green the shade of the skin on king olives, met Nick's gray ones. She looked down first. Why?

She had never used this connection to give a stranger a leg-up before.

"Thanks," Nick said softly. "I'll only use it if I need it, and real easy like."

"I'm sure of it. Or I wouldn't have offered."

A short time later Nick said: "Thanks for everything, Miss Wagner. You did more for me in—minutes—than anybody has in years. I'll go along up to Phipps' place. Had a long drive today and I'd better look bright-eyed and no-beer-smell over at Reed-Farben in the morning."

"You can start calling me Martha. Everybody does. If you don't they won't know who you mean. Tell Abe Phipps I sent you."

"Thanks again. Night."

"Good night—Jim."

Martha Wagner's name was magic with Abe Phipps. Nick drew a cabin in the double line of forty—small, wooden, with ancient plumbing but as clean and shipshape as a Navy cabin. When he washed up he knew by the feel that even the faucet washers were new, smooth flow and no drip.

Some of the cabins were lit, and TV nonsense came softly from some of the screened doors. Nick decided he was far enough from Abe's house so that his comings and goings would not be accurately recorded. When he found the exit at the far end of the cottages, he was certain of it. Abe would need night binoculars, and anyway Nick had noticed the blue glow of Abe's TV screen in the room behind the little office.

He drove slowly past the Reed-Farben plants. When it had been Lyman Electronics there was just the one giant, two-story building in the middle of the plain, modern, window-less, air-conditioned for precision work. The AXE report showed they had gone broke when NASA contracts were not renewed, and that ex-congressman Pearly Abbott (sometimes vilified in opposition pamphlets as "The Pearl of Great Price," the report mentioned) was connected with the Reed-Farben combine which bought the property. A planned double play? Nick wondered.

By the lights, especially the floods at the corners of many of the buildings and the colored spots on the driveways and landscaping, Nick saw the extent of the expansion. The complex was now on three levels. They had put roads up through the bluff and there were houses there. He followed the line of the chain-link fence. It enclosed the operation entirely and, according to the geological map Nick had studied, there were no other entrance roads. That meant the settlement on the bluff had full security; you went in and out at the main gate where cars paused under the bright lights to show their passes.

Standard practice for a war plant. Guards' jobs take up some of the unskilled unemployed and they feel important and vote right. Yet, as Hawk had observed five days ago in Washington, the pieces didn't fit.

Reed-Farben Ltd. was well financed, but the first big bundle had come from Switzerland via Chase, First National City and Bank of California. The combine was wholly owned, the three years of tax reports that were available were in perfect order, and the principals were men of international interests who could never be reached. You talked to their lawyers and accountants.

They produced chemicals, truly enough, but had showed only a bare net profit for the last year. They allegedly had a large R & D—Research and Development Division—working on artificial prosthetic devices. Intricate items—kidneys and implant capsules. Only one interview with a Reed-Farben scientist was to be found in the trade press. A Syrian researcher of note explained in general terms that they were working on prostaglandins. He stated: "Our breakthrough, which is near, scientifically speaking, perhaps two to six years, will mean a form of fine tuning for defective human systems. We work with 16 prostaglandins, chemicals which can alter a function when present in less than one-billionth of a gram. We may be able to offer cures for high blood pressure and defects of the kidneys, brain, lung, thymus, pancreas, iris and reproductive systems."

After Nick read it, Hawk had said: "Sounds like a blooming medicine man's pitch, doesn't it? So we sent Bill Rohde up to Harvard to see Witherspoon. It's all possible. Harvard has similar projects. But—Witherspoon had the same uneasy feeling that got us interested. The pieces don't quite fit.

Reed-Farben people never cross-fertilize with the research community. Never go to trade shows. No advertising except for their standard chemical stuff. Their research staff is largely imported, and they keep to themselves."

"What's this item about a landing strip?" Nick had asked.

"Another oddity. They bought a big executive jet. They built a strip in the valley just over the first mountain behind their plant. Expensive—8,000-foot runway, and usable only in the daytime. We quietly had the general aviation people offer them federal help for landing aids. They're not interested. It's a damn funny business that isn't interested in a handout."

Nick reflected on this conversation as he drove along the twisting highway where it followed a canyon cut leaving the valley. The chain-link fence left the road here—he had seen it when he drove in—and went up the bluff at right angles, enclosing the plant's 180 acres. This did not include the landing strip property, another 520 acres assembled from two former ranches.

There was a turnout along the canyon cut, an ideal place to leave the car. Nick walked back to the fence corner and climbed to where he had noted a gully washed down from the bluff, passing under the fence. Using his flashlight sparingly, he saw a footprint in the wet earth at the side of the ditch and indications that someone—or more than one person—had crawled through. The print was about a size 10. It could have been N82. An easy way in, Nick thought—too easy. With all their security protection, would they overlook this?

Hubie had operated under his own name, as the "probationers" often did on these simple investigative jobs. But if Hubie had been sucked in under that inviting hole in the fence, this might turn into more than a "simple" case. The pieces of the puzzle were showing more and more edges that didn't fit.

Nick had met the redheaded N82 four times, once spent a day with him double shadowing a suspect in Philadelphia. Nick had given the younger man a good mark. The lad was smart, quick and confident. He wanted to make good. Combine that with confidence and you had—a man who would go under a fence to make what he considered a *real* investigation.

Nick drove the thirty miles to Forge Junction, found the Silver Cloud Hotel and parked two blocks away. The town was almost ready for bed; the one movie was letting out, and except for the hotel, a restaurant across the wide main street and three or four bars, the stores were all dark. They didn't waste money here on night window displays.

He put on a brown soft hat, a brown jacket—normally he never wore brown; it was a good color for wrong descriptions —and checked in at the Silver Cloud. He paid in advance and drew Room 26. Hubie had been in 18. The corridor was empty when he went softly along it, unlocked Room 18 after two minutes of experimenting and slipped inside.

Without using lights—small-town hotel people can spot a window wrongly lighted, and Hubie had been gone for several days—Nick searched the room and Hubie's belongings under the glow of his flash. He was quite sure the luggage had been gone over before. Hubie's things were jumbled, but the lad had been neat. The searchers would have found only items to prove that Hubie was a chemical salesman from New York. When Nick discovered that all the music tapes were missing for Hubie's little player, he knew he was right. They had taken them to check at leisure.

Now if Hubie had followed routine and they hadn't found his report. . . . Nick located the Gideon Bible in the back of a bureau drawer. Nestled in a cutout inside its back cover was a tape. AXEmen distribute the Bible with the cutout and dispose of the regular one. They take the AXE one with them when they leave, if they leave—which may account for the statistic that Bibles are the world's most-borrowed books.

Nick pocketed the tape, then checked to make sure he had disturbed nothing.

He opened the door to the hall and a man stepped in front of him. Even in the dim light Nick recognized the weapon that came up from the man's side. A Government model Colt. You didn't hardly get them like that any more. If you have seen what those slugs can do, you stand perfectly still and hope.

"Back in," the man said. Nick backed in.

The man followed him and switched on the room lights. Nick didn't tell him he shouldn't. The man was short and burly, with shoulders wider than Nick's own broad spread, and a flattened nose that had connected too often with fists or gloves—or once with a heavy instrument. The smashed septum was wide. scarred and dented.

"Wha didja git?" His speech fitted his face.

"Who—me? I got into the wrong room."

"Whad areya lookin' for?"

"My room."

"Whatsa number?"

"I thought it was 18."

"Yar. I saw you *pick* 18. Why?"

"I told you."

The gun bobbed impatiently. Nick balanced himself. "You told me nuttin'. Turn around."

"You the house dick?"

"Har har." Even the laugh was ungrammatical. "Yar, I'm the house dick. Now turn around."

Nick said, "Let's talk this over. I didn't take anything. How about a ten spot?"

This struck King Kong as really funny. He laughed again. They teach you in the AXE gymnasium that a laugh often disturbs the focus of the eyes. King Kong grunted as a hand that moved like a striking cobra swept under his gun and lifted. His arm bent at the elbow, was forced up and back over his shoulder. Nick stepped forward and put his weight into the lift and push and press.

An underhand sweep by a man who has practiced it, grabbing a pistol from underneath and forcing the arm up-back-over the shoulder, is an almost irresistible disarming counter. Shoulder and back muscles overpower arm muscles. When the gun hand is well back, the arm jackknifes, and the forefinger—if it is inside the trigger guard—threatens to break. You let go of the gun.

That's the theory. It usually works. It didn't with King Kong. He was short and powerful, and he instinctively pulled down on the gun before Nick carried it past his ear. He dragged it and Nick almost to the floor. Nick made a spear with the fingers of his left hand and jabbed at the side of his opponent's windpipe. He hit a jawbone as rugged as that of the proverbial ass. The two men wrestled for the gun. At the low altitude King Kong had a slight advantage.

Fools tell you—and it's gotten into a few of the man-to-man manuals (but not AXE's)—that an automatic won't fire if you grip the jacket. They even advise to *hold tight*. Don't you believe it.

Or try it—you'll have a paralyzed hand for awhile, if not worse. There *is* some sense in trying to get your hand is front of the hammer of a revolver, unless it's "hammerless," or the hammer of an automatic that has an exposed one. However, if you get down to these technicalities you may be too busy with the overall problem. Nick was.

King Kong found room to swing his left hand, and Nick felt as if a mule had kicked him in the stomach. A large mule. A smaller man, or one not in perfect shape, would have lost his grip on the gun. Nick grunted and heaved upward with both hands, putting his legs and back into it as Mister Solid Beer Barrel hit him again. Nick's haul on his right arm deflected the left. It felt like a smaller mule's kick. He got that right arm further over the man's shoulder and wrestled it down. The gun fell to the floor. They both scrambled for it. King Kong, Mister Beer Barrel—closer to it—reached the weapon first by a quarter-inch. He got a good right-hand grip on it and released the thumb safety. Nick heard the *snick*. BWAM!

The Colt roared parallel to the floor. Nick held the wrist and slugged an edge-of-hand blow to the side of a solid neck. King Kong decided to make it a contest for the gun. They struggled. BWAM! Another slug into the wall.

Nick locked two hands on that wrist, spread and braced his feet, called on larger muscles to overcome his antagonist's smaller ones—back against wrist and arms, now. He turned the Colt into King Kong's belly. They looked at each other, the shorter man staring up at Nick. He paled, his horribly ugly face seeming suddenly childlike and scared, pleading for *something* against terror too mind-shaking to bear. King Kong was remembering what the big .45 slug could do and his intestines were writhing, retreating, going cold.

King Kong was not a coward nor an especially brave man;

he didn't have the perception to go far out either way. Like most men. he was moved by what would happen to his *self* in the immediate future, and right now it looked as if he had no future.

It was a case of a powerful big man against a powerful little man, and the gun stayed in his gut with the muzzle aimed in and up. Nick had automatically maneuvered so that the room's single overhead light was at his back and in King Kong's eyes, which were scared and stayed that way, because the shorter man struggled against the taller one and got nowhere. They swayed and moved a little on the thin carpet like two bulls locked together.

Someone shouted in the hall. A telephone shrilled. Feet thudded on stairs. Nick said, "You want to get out of here alive?"

The bullet head nodded. "Uh." Which must mean yes.

"Let go of the gun and go."

King Kong hesitated.

"You aren't giving up anything," Nick said. "I can belly-shoot you now with a move of my finger.

The short man released his grips and Nick unlocked his own powerful hold on the other's wrist. Nick stepped back with the gun and the other man tore open the door of the room. He ran right over the top of the night clerk who had registered Nick.

He was a tall boy and King Kong left him sprawled all over the hall as if he'd been run over by a galloping horse. He stared up at Nick. "Wh—what's goin' on?" He sat up against the wall as Nick stepped over him, the Colt thrust out of sight in his belt.

"That was her husband. He took a shot at me. Nothing serious." Nick vanished around the corner and flew down the stairs like a ballet dancer.

The little lobby was empty. The stocky man had made fast time. He vanished around a far corner as Nick reached the street. If the local law had been called, it was not in sight. Nick hugged the building to stay out of sight of those who, alerted by the shots, might peek from the hotel windows. The street near his car was deserted. He drove four blocks, made turns, halted in a market's dark parking area to hide the brown jacket and hat in his trunk.

Two miles out of town the road crossed a sharp ravine on a two-lane concrete bridge. Far below water gleamed in a creek in the thin light of the moon and stars. Nick half-stripped the Colt, wiped each part with his handkerchief, and tried to hit that sparkling strip far below, tossing the pieces at different angles.

He passed few cars in Copperpot Valley. Martha's was closed. He rolled into the Alpine and into the parking space beside his cottage with as little noise as possible.

In the cottage, he closed the drapes and set up his cheap little tape player which fed into its counterpart, a cheap radio. They only looked cheap; if you added the cost of their modifications by Stuart, the technical whiz at AXE's laboratories, their price would be substantial. Nick put on the little coil of tape he had found in the Bible and heard Peter, Paul and Mary recorded off a Denver radio station, with Hubie humming once or twice in the background. Nick rerouted the tape and flipped a toggle switch on the back of the set.

Hubie Dumont's voice came through the radio speaker. Nick turned the volume down and listened with his ear at the set.

N82 spoke with little identification, as he had been taught. He said: ". . . key to the subject is the main building. Others are penetrated by local workers. I found no one who has been in the main building, or at least who would admit it. It is especially guarded. I got close to it last night and saw two big men on patrol close in. They may have had a few drinks or been high on drugs. Every two hours the regular security guards loop the building. Yesterday at 1:22 P.M. the plane came in. I was in the woods near the strip. This is the second time my informant has correctly advised about incoming air traffic. Fourteen boxes unloaded and trucked to main building. Five passengers debarked. VIPs, to judge by reception. Met by Doctor Greta Stoltz, Doctor Don Nimura, Kenny Abbott and two men I assume to be executives with subject company. I did not make any of five arrivals, although I had good view through glasses. One man limped, helped, with bandaged face. Other four all Occidentals, Nordic or Slav.

Boxes were assorted sizes, moderate weight. Continuing investigation."

Nick tapped the *Off* button and sat back. He would still bet that "continuing investigation" meant a second trip through that beckoning hole under the Reed-Farben fence. Sucked in—in deep. Those stolid guards could have been part of the come-on. Make it look easy.

The Reed-Farben people listed as meeting the VIP arrivals were all mentioned in the AXE data sheets. Doctors Stoltz and Nimura were researchers. Stoltz had worked in the area of atomic energy for industrial uses—a catch-all job description—but Nimura, who was an M.D. to Greta Stoltz's Ph.D., had been working on heart and kidney transplants in Japan before he came to Colorado.

Nick took a warm shower, then rubbed alcohol on his wrist where King Kong had gripped it and on his hand where the Colt had bruised it. The night was warm, the air balmy with pine scent. His cottage was far enough back from the highway so that the occasional car or truck passing by did not intrude on the rustic atmosphere. A pleasant change after the cities. Why did people have to mess up nice places like this with their greed and angle shooting?

The atmosphere changed abruptly about 7 A.M. A parade of growling, honking cars and trucks packed the highway. Reed-Farben Ltd. ran on two shifts in most departments, the first starting at 8 A.M. Nick discovered a truck terminal across the road from the Alpine—that didn't help. Nor did a small metal barrel plant adjacent to the motel. They apparently reclaimed and refinished barrels, by the hundreds, each one with a *bang-crash-hiss-splat* as it was cleaned, scraped and spray painted. No wonder Abe Phipps offered thrifty rates.

Nick drove eight miles west to Deadwood Dick's Trading Post for breakfast. Over orange juice, steak and eggs and coffee—no bread—he thought over N82's moves, and his own like a chess master reviewing a game. N82 had moved logically and efficiently, though perhaps overconfidently. He thought about Martha Wagner. Warm, attractive—and smart. Whatever was going on here, she knew something about it, even if she didn't know she knew. She was used to rambling itinerants like Jim Perry. They did not move logically. It would be illogical if they did!

Nick bought a roast beef sandwich and two apples. He selected an old road on his geological map of 1931—it turned out to be an old mine road—and parked his car at the end of it. Carrying a cheap camera, he spent the day circling the mountains surrounding the Reed-Farben valley and the air strip beyond. He discovered old abandoned roads, a railroad right-of-way stripped of its tracks and an empty farmhouse.

He watched through binoculars as the residents of Reed-Farben's private community came and went. There were wives and children, and a yellow school bus came in about 3 P.M. It had to pass through the front gate like all the cars and trucks.

Slowly he moved the binoculars to cover the buildings where Reed-Farben's business was conducted. A truck backed into one. Nick's field glasses stayed with the boxes being unloaded by a crew of three, under the watchful eye of a white-coated Japanese.

The Japanese said something to the men; one of them, obviously annoyed, stopped working to answer back. The Japanese gestured impatiently, his hands making "hurry up" motions. The men speeded up their work. Suddenly, a box dropped, its covering flying off to one side, contents spilling crazily all over the ground.

Nick's eyebrows shot up in surprise. Hands—perfectly formed, grotesquely real—spilled from the box. Some were knotted into a tight fist, ready to deliver a sharp blow; others curled around an invisible object, straining to maintain their grip.

The men stared dumbly about. Nick's powerful binoculars picked up their shock so clearly he could have been standing right next to them. Only the Japanese doctor had kept his head. He reached down and put the grisly things back into their box. His lips were silently counting as he returned the pieces.

The truckers continued to stare, two of them exchanging uneasy glances. They obviously had no idea what they had been told to load. The Japanese leaned down for the box's lid and clamped it back on.

The unloading resumed. The Japanese pushed a button at

the side of the building and another white-coated figure hurried out. The two spoke for a short while, then the second doctor disappeared inside Within five minutes he was back, a slight bulge in one of his coat pockets, the top of the package showing above the flap.

He sauntered over to the cab of the truck. The Japanese walked to the back of the vehicle where the men were working; he was watching them very intently now. The second doctor lifted the hood of the truck, transferred the package from his pocket inside the motor, then gingerly closed the hood. Nick was pretty sure the truckers never saw him. Nick felt a trickle of sweat meander down his neck.

In less than an hour the three men climbed into the truck and it pulled away, heading for a far corner of the Reed-Farben plant. Nick was not quite ready for the loud. sharp blast that tore the giant vehicle apart. Flames leaped to the sky from the truck's motor. bits and pieces of steel flew into the air then slammed into the ground. Nick thought he saw a head, blood running from the eyes. soar on high. He shook his own head clear and put the binoculars down.

He couldn't figure it The murder of the three men had gone so smoothly. it must have been done according to a prearranged plan. Get rid of anybody who might know anything But why? What the hell were they hiding? Why take such enormous risks?

He got back to his car at 6:30 and drove to Martha's Diner. He stood at the bar until he could get the booth next to her private one, and ordered the chef's special—beef goulash. She found him as he was finishing rice pudding and coffee, and stopped by his booth and smiled.

"Hi, Jim. How'd it go?"

"Go? Uh—what go?"

"At the personnel office."

"Oh." He let his eyes leave hers and said, "Aw, I didn't get to it today. I went up into the mountains. It was such a nice day. I didn't get back in time. I'll go tomorrow."

She settled slowly into the seat opposite, looking at him like a fond mother. It worked so perfectly that he felt guilty, kept his eyes on his coffee cup.

"I guess you needed a day's rest after your trip," she said, "but you ought to get over there tomorrow for sure. Jobs don't wait, you know, and you might have just missed one. Have another coffee?"

Nick had another coffee, then two beers, and was moved into Martha's booth. He was being mothered. A role that will take you a long, long way with almost any woman, but a difficult one to play. You become the son, with little weaknesses that can be changed, and loved for your virtues. When Martha bounced out of the booth now and then he watched the way her firm, ample body moved. Those were muscles under those curves— hard work kept her in condition.

"I'd offer to drive you home," Nick said shyly, "but I suppose you have your own car."

She looked at him thoughtfully, thinking, you're a handsome rascal, travelin' man. She wondered why. He didn't act like a boozer—she had a nose and an eye for them, after years with Pete. He probably had just been turned loose and never found an anchor. She said, "Want to take a little guided tour?"

"I'd like it very much."

"C'mon." That's a big part of it, she decided, the guy is lonely. He won't be for long once that corn-fed herd of fillies at Reed-Farben get a look at him.

Martha's car was a Lincoln Continental convertible, gleaming black in the lights of the rear lot. They purred west on the highway and she said, "This car is my big luxury. I drove wrecks so long that when I could—well—"

"You deserve it." Nick answered. "The way you work you deserve a lot, Martha. I mean—a lot of girls in your position wouldn't be so kind to—a truckdriver."

"Nothing wrong with truckdriving if you don't let it be your dead end. We have a couple of them who go to the University of Colorado in winter. You don't even look like a truckdriver, Jim. What did you do before that Monongahela job?"

"Installer for Western Union on the microwaves. That's when I took that ski vacation up here. I was super of a gang when I quit."

"Why did you quit? That was a good spot."

"Always on the move. Our next job was in California."

Martha laughed. "So you don't really like to ramble?"

"No, I don't think so. Things just worked that way." Nick sighed. "This is the kind of country I'd like to settle in."

Martha drove well. They swooped along the cliff-edge roads with easy turns and no chances. A couple of miles beyond the trading post she turned off the main road and followed a gravel track that climbed steeply. It circled and twisted its way up between pines, and suddenly they were on an open ledge with a view for miles. The mountains were jagged outlines in the moonlight. Far below and far away lights twinkled. It was like passing over the area in a plane.

Martha parked facing the precipice. "This was the road to Lost Goat Mine but it's washed out up above here. Look at those lights way off there. You can see for fifty miles."

"It's great," Nick said. "But I don't usually park on a first date."

She laughed with him, handed him a cigarette. He held a match before she could find the lighter. "You're safe, man," she replied. "I don't often park at all. I guess I really brought you up here to ask you something. I want your promise. . . ."

"Well, now. My mother warned me about nights like this and I promised her I'd walk home if I had to. But it's a long walk and I'd probably get lost and fall over a cliff or something. On the other hand, I'm just a youngster and——"

"Stop that." She crossed her left hand over and found a ticklish spot in his ribs. He gasped, laughed and twisted Wilhelmina further back under his armpit. She had nearly touched the gun. "Be serious, Jim. It's important."

He turned and leaned until his nostrils touched her hair. It smelled marvelous. "You have lovely hair. Do you have to drive to Denver to a beauty parlor?"

"No. Annie Parker in Highland does beautiful work. But never mind my hair; I want to talk about you. Where did you go today instead of looking for that job?"

His alert mind considered possibilities. Was Martha checking on him for someone else? He decided to trust a hunch and his usually good judgment of people. "Nowhere important. I just felt tired, I guess, after traveling up here. I walked around the mountains."

"Do you feel rested now?"

"Sure." He stroked the muscle of her right arm, a feathery, friendly touch. "And thanks for taking an interest in me, Martha. It makes me feel—nice. A little important to some-one."

"Then you'll do something for me—and yourself?"

"Maybe. What?"

"See about that job tomorrow. Don't put it off. Make up your mind to get there early and put your best foot forward. Promise?"

"I promise." He felt a small warm glow. This girl saw them come and go, by the hundreds, and he was sure she husbanded her emotions and her affection carefully. She was helping Jim Perry because she saw something in him she liked, and it was nice to be liked, even if your name was Nick Carter instead of Jim Perry. She liked the man, not the name.

"Thank you," she whispered. "We all like to put things off—"

The breeze through the windows was piney scented. A nightbird called ooh-ooh and another answered.

"Are you—were you—ever married?" Martha asked. Then she frowned in the gloom. That was an awkward question. Why had it slipped out?

"Just nearly, once," Nick replied. That was near the truth. "After that—I guess I've been on the move too much." Which was the truth.

Yes, she told herself, he would be like that. Hurt would go deep with him; you could tell he was sensitive under that pre-tense of not-a-care-in-the-world. He kept moving because he wasn't going to let his emotions expose him again.

Martha's sublimated need for affection churned inside her. She stopped wondering why she was so attracted to this strangely gentle man and sighed. She felt warm and wanted, and yet actually in command. She had gotten used to running things, in a treadmill of long hours and hard work, letting it smother her vital need for friendship—for passion.

Nick put his big hand over hers. He massaged it softly,

then turned over her palm. The friction of his rubbing was warm, tingly, companionably intimate. She thought, he's hesitant, cautious with women the way he's reluctant to enter a new situation like asking for a job. Somebody ought to help him. He's worth it. You can tell he has good, solid qualities under that hurt veneer.

It took him a long time to put his arms around her, so that when he did she was impatient to be held and kissed and fondled. She wanted to help him relax, she told herself, and let him discover how delightful a genuine friendship could be. To restrain him was the last thing in her mind; she would decide when that was necessary and act accordingly. He kissed her and his lips were as she guessed they would be, tender and patient. She snuggled against him with a humming sigh.

A very special girl, Nick decided. It was more than the savory aroma and firm-warm feel of her; he formed his opinion on the whole picture of the last two days.

He fondled her and she joined in the pleasant, lazy game. When his lips reached her nipples, which he had deftly bared as if it were the obvious thing to do, she decided it was time to put on the brakes. She was wondering what tactic to use when he opened his door and they were half lying on the seat.

"No," she murmured.

Instantly the warm pressure on her relaxed and she felt both reassured and deprived. Looking dreamily upward, she saw two stars. Their golden flickers seemed to be only inches from the dark outline of his strong jaw and high cheekbone. She giggled.

"What's the matter?"

"The stars—"

"In my eyes?"

"No. Around your face. There are two bright ones trying to make you look like—like an angel."

"It would take more than stars," he said softly, and looked up. The cloud cover had opened and in the clear mountain air the masses of stars were magnificent. They formed a full ceiling of glimmering specks and nuggets. "Beautiful," he said.

She sighed and moved a little and she enjoyed the way he

fitted against her—so lightly, yet with a complete kind of tin-
gling warmth that caused her skin to glow in response. The
warmth was more than skin deep, she decided as he kissed her
again. She could feel it somewhere in her throat, and in her
chest—would you call it in the heart?—and all along her spine.

Suddenly she said, "Oh—oh—" dragging the words slowly
out on long breaths.

Martha flamed suddenly with the intensity of a person de-
nied water until the suffering need is irresistible. She put a
hand inside his shirt and pulled up cloth and reveled in the
touch of his warm flesh. Her hand moved down, opening his
belt buckle and the zipper of his slacks. She shuddered as she
explored him. She thrust her tongue deep into his mouth and
writhed against him as if desperate for closer contact.

Her buttocks moved on the cushions, side to side, with a
steady rhythm. Her skirt had worked its way almost to her
waist, and he traced patterns on the inside of her thighs with
dancing fingers. He unhooked her stockings from her garter
and she lifted herself so he could push her panties off.

He entered her swiftly and easily. She gave little gasps, her
breath beating moist and sweet into his nostrils. Then she
moved her head slightly so her tongue could penetrate his ear,
moved down to give small, sharp bites to his neck. Her sturdy
rump was pinioned in the V of the seat, but her body kept up
its even rhythm.

She moaned. Once, when he reached far inside her, she gave
a short, shrill scream. He stayed with her steady pace, kept it
even as she increased her own tempo beneath him. She raised
her legs high in the air, then lifted her hips, straining against
him.

His hands clutched her buttocks, one finger stroking the
softness between. His body moved with smooth, unbroken
strokes as he kneaded her smooth, warm flesh. He could feel
his own breath, harsh and guttural.

He was in command now, the total master. She lay almost
still, her body trembling from his assault. He was moving faster,
faster, stronger all the time, riding the crest of passion, time-
less and eternal.

He moved forward on the seat, his head up, his body in quick, savage thrusts. Somewhere, far away, he thought she was whispering something, a soft "God . . . darling . . . oh . . ." Her hands tightened about him, fingers digging deep into his back. The pressure was building and there was the heat washing over both of them.

Nick licked away tears that trickled down her cheeks. He was fairly sure that Martha Wagner never cried at sex and at not much else—but this was one of those right times at the right place with (he felt an odd pleasure at the idea) the right man. He realized that his own breathing tempo was catching up with hers; the gusty, reflex ins and outs. He ran his tongue along her lower lip and she quivered with delight and caught him in a warm, tender trap. One set of her fingernails flexed on the skin of his right hip and the other clasped at him near an armpit like the quills of an aroused but not angry little animal.

He held her tightly and knew, as he had partly guessed, that he had discovered something unusual and rare. Worth preserving. She was drawing on him inexorably, their joined course down a rushing, thrilling stream no more reversible than that of a light canoe in millrace rapids. But there was no sense of danger, just a great lift of release. The fluid that bore them came from hot springs and these were rapids without rocks and certain to end in a warm, languid pool.

He paused, floating through a calm with muscles stilled for an instant by a great effort of command. He raised his head, listened for sounds that didn't belong in the night, heard nothing. This was rare, and he knew that for a few moments he would be unaware, his always alert antenna devoted to one channel of energy. It would be welcome. He knew value when he felt it, and in a society where honest communication between man and woman has become so difficult, this should be savored.

He raised a hand higher on her bare back, pressing her against him as he increased the speed of their shared voyage again. She matched his strokes with small delighted sounds of approval. They went through the warm rapids and flashed along the canyon, sharing a marvelous trip, committed now to climaxing the joyous voyage, neither able nor wanting to stop or turn back.

After their first vigor was expended and they floatetd in the warm pool he knew how right he had been. It was very special, and he considered himself a man of enough experience and judgment to know. You could tell, and this in itself required experience, that they had both been honest—all the way.

He rested his weight largely on the cushions, listening to the soft decline of her breaths, feeling the ebb of his own pulse, so strong he could hear the tiny beat in his ears. It was a long time before she said, "That was—surprisingly nice, Jim—"

He kissed her nose and forehead as a sign of agreement. After another long pause she said, "I like this too. But my left leg has gone to sleep."

He withdrew, backing carefully past the steering wheel and massaged her legs tenderly. She sighed with satisfaction. "Take the keys," she said softly. "Did you ever take a dip in a warm mountain pool?"

"Just a minute ago" he replied. "I was in a magic canoe with you and we went down friendly rapids and there we were. And we seemed to be floating in it as much as on it. As if the canoe swam with us."

"I felt—sort of like that, too. But I mean really. Come on—"

She slid out of the car and in the ghostly moon-and-star light he saw her remove her skirt and blouse. She sat on the edge of the seat and stripped off her stockings. "Take your clothes off," she ordered. "You'll be surprised—"

Dutifully he undressed. He retrieved Wilhelmina from under the seat and wrapped it in his trousers. "O.K. Show me. I'll carry my pants, though, with my wallet and the keys."

"Good idea. Come on." She took his hand and headed, sure-footed, through the gorse away from the cliff.

He followed, discovering that the dim view of her nude body, which seemed to develop a soft glow all its own when they passed through areas where no trees blocked the faint light from the night sky, gave him a pleasant stimulation. When it's honest, he thought, your energy comes back fast.

"I thought all these mountain streams were cold," he said.

"This isn't a stream. It's a tank of stone. A little spring feeds it and it slops over so slowly it stays warm. That is, as long as there's some sun during the day. Careful now—there isn't much of a trail—" She guided him up a ridge of shale. "We don't mark the path and the rocks are hard to climb. But it's good—it keeps the tourists from finding it."

They topped the rock ridge and he saw water gleaming in the moonlight. Nestled in the stone was a pool, perhaps thirty feet across, with a stand of small firs on its far side. Martha took off her shoes and pulled at his hand. "Come on. Take your shoes off. It's warm. And deep."

It was. He was surprised at the soothing, almost oily feel of the water as they swam across and climbed out on the ledge beneath the firs. He said, "Man, that's great. There must be a warm spring under it."

"I don't know. Perhaps. It never really freezes."

He walked back around the tank and brought his trousers and their shoes to the soft patch of earth and sat down beside her. She said, "I've got a bottle and cigarettes in the car, Jim. I forgot about them. They didn't seem—needed."

"They're not," he answered, and turned and enfolded her in his arms. They kissed and relaxed back onto the fallen needles.

When he ran his lips down her neck to capture a nipple she murmured, "No, Jim. I don't think we should—we shouldn't have—and not again—"

Her hand slid down his hard belly and she gasped.

She objected once again, a few feeble and futile words which she forgot all about, apparently, very quickly.

The burly man Nick had tangled with back at Forge and dubbed King Kong drove up to the Reed-Farben gatehouse and stopped under the lights. The guard inspected his ID card, nodded recognition. The man drove in, parked his Mercury in the lot at the main building, and went through the ID check again inside the big doors. He waited about ten minutes before Kenny Abbott came for him.

Kenny looked like a modern corporate junior executive, moving with the brisk, important steps and motions meant to indicate purposefulness, but because they're so continuously automatic they have no more conviction than the jerky hops of a puppet. He wore the dark suit and small-figured tie, looked at you with the keen open-closed expression, and his mouth dropped into a hard pout when it didn't wear the fixed half smile or you caught him unaware, especially from the side. His eyes opened extra wide when he looked at you but narrowed when he believed he wasn't observed.

Most people believed him and trusted him, unless they had been around the type and had been bitten.

"Hello, Joe," Kenny said. "Everything okay?"

The burly man mumbled a greeting and walked beside him through the second barrier doors and along a wide corridor. He failed to meet Kenny's practiced open glance, but Abbott wasn't alerted. Joe never looked you in the eye. "Yah," Joe said. "I searched the room. Nuttin'. Anudder guy showed up. I braced him. Nuttin'."

"He came to the room?"

"Yar."

"You'd better tell Mr. Benn about it."

Joe sniffed timidly as they passed doors which led into the big rooms. He always told himself he wasn't scared of anything in the world, but the mixture of smells you got here made his back hairs prickle. It was like the dentist's office after he opened an abscess. Joe had gotten a look through one of the doors, once. It looked like a giant hospital, all white tile and stainless steel and people in white coats.

They entered a large office. Mr. Benn was behind the desk, wearing the gauze mask. Joe noticed he never lifted up his right arm. Crippled? Maybe he had none. Benn was the big wheel. What he said went. A real big shot. He flew in and out as if a private jet was a taxi.

Joe wondered about the man who had had Room 18 at the Silver Cloud Hotel in Forge Junction. He had asked around. He wondered if Mr. Benn had had him taken care of. Benn would do it. Joe had seen the type—or a similar type—before. Smart. Talked nice. But look out. Remembering what had really happened in Room 18, Joe was worried.

Kenny Abbott said, "Joe saw a man at that hotel room, Mr. Benn."

"Ah." The eyes above the gauze mask were cold and hard. The voice with its accent tried to be genial. "Tell me about it, Joseph."

"Well, I searched the joint and found nuttin'. Like I said when I called in. So I got this room up the hall like and I watched the room like I was told to. Nuttin' for three days. I was gonna quit the stakeout that night like I was told; then this guy showed up. He opened the door with a passkey and went in. He put the bolt on behind him, so I waited till he started to come out and then I braced him. He was a soft shoe man. Thought I was the hotel dick and tried to bribe me. I put on an act, and the clerk knocked on the door so I got out of there."

Silence. The eyes above the mask were like a pair of car headlights in a thick fog. Joe swallowed. Benn said, "Kenny, please leave us alone for a few minutes."

Kenny went out. Joe shifted his weight from foot to foot. Geez, this guy could get under your skin. Hell, he wasn't so tough. Just an old crip. It must be him mixed with the smell of the place that did it.

"Describe the man," Benn said softly.

"Uh, big. Over six feet. Mebbe 220 pounds. Brown eyes, brownish skin. Brown suit. Black hat." Joe didn't really remember; he made it up.

"You searched him to see if he found anything?"

"Uh—sure."

"Then you let him go to avoid a disturbance?"

"Yar." Joe thought tensely, he don't believe me. He could tell. He had watched a lot of these big shots since he had left the coal mines to work for a strike-breaking outfit. A professional thug he met on the job in the copper country put him wise to the fact that he was now a detective. He had worked for a detective agency, hadn't he? Joe liked the idea.

Somehow he never lasted long anywhere as a "detective." People were against him, he decided, because he was a hunkie. Then Pearly Abbott had lined him up with Reed-Farben through his nephew, Kenny. First telling Joe, "I'd like to know exactly what goes on there, Joe my boy, and I'll make

sure you're well paid for your extra time and trouble." Joe
knew all about Pearly. The old politician would steal a red-
hot stove even if he had no gloves or potholders. Joe liked
the arrangement—a payoff from two sides and no taxes on
the money from Pearly. The trouble was, Joe found out so
little about Reed-Farben he had to make up lots of stories for
Pearly, and his imagination wasn't that great.

Mr. Benn was silent so long Joe got scared. He don't believe me! Has the bastard got a gun under that desk? Some of
these old nuts can be dangerous and this one looks like the
worst kind.

"Now, Joe," Mr. Benn said softly, "I want you to take on
a very special job for me. Did you get a good look at the
man's face?"

Joe knew Benn had been going to accuse him of lying but
had changed his mind. "Sure. We was right under the light
together for four-five minutes."

"Was he an athletic type? You said tall, heavy, but was he
—graceful?"

"Yar. Yar, I'd say so."

"He'll be around here again, I'm sure. You'll find him, I
think, if you just spend time around that diner and the trading post and the mine stores. Certainly you ought to visit the
village every day or so. Just keep looking. He'll come."

"Sure. I guess."

"I'll pay you a nice bonus when you find him. Say—four
hundred dollars."

"If he comes in smellin' distance I'll get him, Mr. Benn."
Joe grinned and nodded. He wondered what kind of accent
the man had. All he could think of was hunkie, like the
squareheads up around the mines back home. But that wasn't
just it. The guy wasn't especially big but with those cold eyes
gleaming over that mask and that right arm that never
showed—he gave you the creeps. Betcha ten that right hand
holds a cannon.

Joe couldn't know that there was no hand there, but the
complex metal substitute was holding a gun—or rather part
of the stainless steel assembly was a gun, pointed right at
Joe's belly.

"Here is something nicer," Benn said. "If you kill him, or

capture him and bring him here, I'll pay you twenty times as much and send you to a beautiful town on the sunny Mediterranean for a year. At full pay. Would you like that?"

"Yar! If he's near this state I'll find him."

"When you do, my advice is this . . . you don't mind my giving a professional like you advice, do you, Joseph?"

Joe Felix's head waggled rapidly from side to side. Negative signal.

"Get him alone. If you could follow him until night, that would be ideal. Don't try to capture him. Don't even talk to him. Shoot him in the back. Several times, to be sure. You won't have any problems, because all you have to do is come here and I'll have you flown away. Rich. In my personal jet."

Joe glowed. "I get the picture, Mr. Benn."

CHAPTER II

Nick was at the Reed-Farben personnel office at nine the next morning. He wore green cotton work pants and a shirt to match, and a mismatched gray sweater-jacket. He carried a pair of horsehide-faced work gloves and his shoes were laced ones, ankle high. A Teamster's Union button rode on the side of his khaki cap. It was an actor's getup, clean and neat and perfect for the part.

A pretty, empty-faced brunette put on her bright smile for him and gave him long forms to fill out. He carefully inscribed the details of his truckdriver's background, as set up by AXE, using the Alpine address and telephone number for his local residence. When he turned in the forms the brunette said, "Thank you. We'll call you if there's an opening."

Ouch. Don't call us, we'll call you. He lowered his glance to the desk top and said, "I was told I oughta ask for Mr. Kenneth Abbott. He might have somethin'."

"Oh. Just a minute—" She picked up her phone and pressed a button. "Hi—Mary Ann? There's a truckdriver here was referred to Mr. Abbott." Pause. "Huh huh—" Brown eyes swimming in too much green dye caught his. "Who told you to see Mr. Abbott?"

He put on the frank, boyish look. "Miss Martha Wagner."

The brunette relayed the information, listened, hung up. "Please have a seat. Mr. Abbott will see you in a little while —I think."

The little while became an hour. Nick read a copy of *Look*, saw his application forms picked up by a messenger, watched seven applicants appear, sweat over forms, and depart with the "We'll call you if there's an opening" dismissal.

At 10:19 the brunette answered her phone, then guided him through two doors and along a short hall and handed him over to another girl. Mary Ann, he decided. She was a carbon copy of the brunette, with differently tinted hair. She conducted him in to meet the well-groomed Kenny Abbott.

Abbott didn't get up or put out his hand. He gestured at a chair in front of his desk. Nick saw his application in front of the man. Abbott looked at him carefully. "How long have you known Martha Wagner?"

"Not very long, Mr. Abbott. She cashes my checks."

"I see. Why'd you come to Colorado?"

"I've been here before. I like the country."

Kenny pretended to study Nick's application. Because he was an astonishingly devious man himself, he tried to read more into Nick's replies than was there. They were the kind of answers he would have given if he had more clout than he wanted to expose. He knew Martha quite well. This was the first man she had ever recommended.

More important, he knew that his Uncle Pearly knew her extremely well—did he get into her from time to time?—and he didn't want to annoy Pearly in the slightest. Pearly had put him here, in a lousy ten-thousand-a-year job when he needed twice that to live the way he wanted to. Pearly was as devious as a computer's circuits. His angles had angles. Kenny was working on Benn and Rick and the rest to develop some angles of his own—you didn't want to make mistakes at a time like this. Even a little jiggle would upset the gravy bowl, and you would lose out.

This guy—he glanced at the form, Jim Perry—this Perry wouldn't be a bad-looking man if you put him in decent clothes. Big body. Martha didn't have a steady man. Could that be it? She was interested in this yokel personally and Pearly had nothing to do with it? Still—if he offended Martha and she squawked to Pearly—

"Mr. Perry, we check references *very* carefully. Are you willing to have us call your previous employers and the other men you've listed?"

"Certainly. I got a good work record. No accidents."

"Can you get local union clearance?"

Nick lifted up his cap and pointed to the button. "No sweat." Let Kenny call every reference. If he didn't get clean okays on "Jim Perry" AXE should go out of business. When they set something up it held together.

"I don't know if we need another driver," Pearly's nephew said, testing. "We only use about fifteen tractors of our own and most of it is hauling trailers to Denver where they're loaded on U.P. or Santa Fe Railroad cars. You know how to handle them?"

"I've moved plenty of railvans and Flexis," Nick lied easily. "I really need a job, Mr. Abbott. I'll go on spare."

Kenny sighed. This guy was either smoother than he looked or he knew he could run whining to Martha or Pearly and put on some pressure. "Wait outside, Mr. Perry. Let me see what I can do."

Nick found his way back to the personnel lobby. In twenty minutes the brunette gave him more forms, took his social security number, gave him a silly talk about Reed-Farben being a great place to work and described all the benefits he would enjoy. He left with instructions to report to the traffic manager at four the next afternoon.

Because he was already past the entrance gate, Nick drove the Ford along the side of the main building, studying it across the hundred feet of lawn, and then found his way to the loading docks behind the newer, oblong factories.

These were the units that produced Reed-Farben's commercial chemicals and pharmaceutical products—the division that showed a nice profit on the balance sheets. If they had set up these operations to cover whatever they were up to, they had hit on lines that promptly turned in a handsome income. Pearly's influence in getting government orders for the stuff undoubtedly helped. It could be a case of the cover financing the illicit business. It smelled wrong, but you had to weigh all factors.

The trucks at the dock were a mixture. Macks, GMs and some Internationals. Nick shrugged. He could handle them. AXEmen were checked out on almost everything that moved, including PT boats and twin-engine planes.

The dock supervisor was a harried little man with a bald head and a day-old growth of white whiskers. Nick got him for a moment and said, "My name's Jim Perry. S'posed to come on at four tomorrow."

Baldy paused, wiped sweat from his gleaming dome. "Good." His eyes were red and watery but missed nothing. He spotted the Teamster's button. "I'm Rainey. Drivers I got. Mountain kids. But I need help with the tiedowns. You know 'em?"

"Container vans? Sure."

"Awright. Will you gimme a hand tomorrow? Then you can take a load to Denver."

Nick thought fast. Why was he asking? Then he got it—Rainey was short of experienced men and wanted to bend the union rules a little. "Sure."

"Okay, Jim. See you on the second shift. We—"

A roller conveyor that was feeding cartons into a trailer got away from the two men handling it. Cartons spilled all over the dock. Rainey spun away with a last, "See you tomorrow."

When Nick reached his Ford a plant patrol car was parked near it. The guard, a brown-faced overweight type, said, "Where's your plant tag?"

"I was just hired."

"Oh. You can't drive anywhere but between the gate and the visitor's parking lot till you have a tag."

"Sorry. Where do I get my tag?"

"When you starting?"

"Tomorrow."

"It'll be at the gate office."

"Thanks." Nick drove back to the gatehouse and out to the highway. They certainly ran the operation by the numbers.

He drove to Martha's and got coffee and a bran muffin. Martha had not yet arrived. He pulled out the little folder the brunette had given him. On the cover it said, WELCOME TO REED-FARBEN . . . A GOOD PLACE TO WORK.

He read it swiftly. After outlining the good life that was ahead for him, the last page warned, "Don't talk. Your company is engaged in very secret government work in addition to our domestic product production. Remember, the enemy is everywhere. No communist looks like one. Be watchful and don't—don't talk."

There was a spot picture of a man at a lunch counter with two others leaning toward him from each side. They had oversize ears. As art work, Nick thought it was a dead loss.

In the big diner it was that quiet moment between breakfast and lunch when there is a noticeable pause before the noon rush. Peter Wagner, looking tense and irritated, slammed shut the cash drawer he had been checking and went behind the bar and drew a small beer. He came over to the booth where Nick sat—the special booth.

"Hello, Jim." He slid into the seat. "What a morning! Meat truck late, two waitresses won't show and the damn cash account is nine bucks out—on the plus side yet. Then I get a call a bus tour wants to stop here for lunch tomorrow. Fifty-two people and we gotta rush the order for them. Steaks all around." He drank a third of the small glass of beer.

"Some days it don't pay to get up," Nick replied. That was about what a bored truckdriver might say. He felt like pointing out that around the world men were sweating, suffering, worrying, dying. They looked at hopeless hours in jails and hospitals. A third of a billion were hungry or half starved. Pete was wearing good clothes, he had a decent car, money in his kick, a full belly—and *he* was complaining.

Nick suppressed a grimace. He liked Pete. The man had a lot of Martha's solid qualities. Probably he was smarter than his sister, in a way, but he was also more nervous, impetuous, quick to act. Be kind, Nick reminded himself, everyone you meet carries a heavy load.

"You get the job?" Pete asked.

"Start tomorrow."

"Do you like driving trucks?"

"I guess so. You see the country. Not the same scene all the time, like in a factory."

Pete drained his beer, went over to the bar and drew himself a refill. From the corner of his eye Nick saw Bob Half-Crow's black, inscrutable eyes follow Pete. You couldn't read their expression, but the fact that they stayed on the younger Wagner from booth to pump to booth told you what might be in the mind behind them.

Pete sat down, drank half the little glass. "You know anything about that outfit?"

"What outfit?"

"Reed-Farben. Your new boss."

"Just what they told me," Nick said. "The usual guff. I'm starting on the railvans to Denver." He handed Pete the folder the brunette had given him. Pete riffled pages with his thumb, checked a few lines and gave it back.

"I've read it. It's what isn't in there that fascinates me, Jimmy boy. Wanna make a little deal?"

"I'm always open," Nick answered cautiously.

Pete lowered his voice. "You know I'm a newspaperman. I mean, I'm up here helping Martha, but someday I'll go back—"

Nick nodded. Pete didn't know that Nick knew his history —fired from three papers for boozing.

"There's a story there," Pete said. He emptied his glass, forgot to pitch his voice extra low but it still didn't carry beyond the booth. "That outfit has either got something new that'll rock the industry and make millions, or they're phony as a thirty-dollar bill. Sure they make chemicals and pharmaceuticals, but what do they make in the old Lyman building, eh? Do you know?"

"No." Nick shook his head, replied in a whisper, leaned forward, opened his eyes wide. "What?"

Pete laughed. A short bark. "Nobody knows. If you can find out or even get a lead, I'll explore it, and when we get enough info I'll write up an article. If I get any dough for it I'll split with you."

"What'll I look for?" Nick asked smoothly. "You must have some idea."

"I have." Pete's face was redder than it had been when he sat down. He took his empty glass to the bar, dropped it into the bar sink—you could hear the gulping plop—and drew himself another beer, using a twelve-ounce shell glass. He came back. Nick feared that if Bob Half-Crow put a few more volts in his glance Pete might be electrocuted.

Pete gulped beer. He could really pour it down. "You bet I have. They've got chemical and medical experts there from all over the world. Equipment goes in and out of there as if it's the Mayo Clinic being rebuilt. They built an airstrip just to fly stuff in and out and nobody knows where some of the stuff comes from or goes to. Their security setup is weird. They're as tough on their own people as they are on the public."

Nick pretended to be puzzled. "Huh?"

"Sure." Pete leaned forward. He was getting the red-faced wise-owl look. "The natives who work in the production plants never see the inside of the main building. At night there's a special force of secret guards around it. Where do they come from? They don't live around here. And the quickest way to get fired is to get nosy." Nick was astonished to see that the large glass was empty.

"What about the cleaners, janitors?" Nick asked. "They oughta get pieces of the puzzle."

"Never happen. All that crew lives up in the fancy compound."

"Get to 'em when they come down for a night out."

"They never do. They don't even talk to the natives. When they go out they go to Denver or beyond. Some of their kids take the school buses, but you can't get much out of children. Especially since I'll betcha they don't know anything."

Nick nodded, showing interest. "I'll keep my eyes open, Pete, but what makes you think I'll get a chance to find out anything?"

"You've been around, Jim. You've got more head on you than the usual truckdriver. I'm betting you haven't spent your whole life behind a diesel. Maybe you'll just get a scrap here and there. Maybe a peek at a shipment. If there's a pattern to be discovered, between us I'll bet we can find it. Is it a deal?" He put out a hand. It shook a little.

Nick took the smaller man's hand, almost puny beside his own. But Pete's grip was firm, the palm hard. "I'll try," Nick said.

"Good." Pete grinned and headed for the bar with his glass. His face was flushed. Nick decided he was one of those who showed it quickly, carried it a long time, and could drink for several days before wavering and collapsing.

Bob Half-Crow, posed like a grim brown statue near the service bar, suddenly turned, swung around the mahogany drop gate and came over to Nick. The Indian spoke for

Nick's ears alone. "He's trouble when he drinks. Try and slow him down, or get him out. For Martha."

Martha came in from the front entrance, looking lovely in a tailored blue suit as she made her way through the gathering noon crowd in the bar. She caught Pete in the middle of the room as he headed back toward the booth, carrying the foaming glass like a chalice. They both froze for an instant. Nick felt sorry for them. You could feel the anger, frustration and helplessness.

Martha followed her brother to the booth, but the swing was gone from her walk, the radiance from her face. "Morning, Jim."

Nick gave her his own best cheerup expression. "Good morning, Martha. You look great."

"Thanks."

A dead silence. Pete took a long drink of beer with a gesture that couldn't help looking defiant. Nick felt as if he were watching a TV show—not a good one. He knew the background because he had watched the first scenes and the players didn't know he knew. Pete the alcoholic threatening to ride the tiger again, Martha the patient sister hoping for the best and knowing she'd get the worst, Bob Half-Crow the loyal family friend, willing to baby Pete or batter him and knowing that neither would work. Nick recalled the technical definition of alcoholism—a physical allergy coupled with a mental compulsion.

The place was starting to jump. The clock above the bar read one minute before noon. Pete said, "I better get on the gate. Remember what I said, Jim."

"Sure," Nick replied. Pete went forward to the U-shaped counter fronting the doors, taking the remains of his beer with him.

"What did he say?" Martha asked.

"He thinks there might be a news story in Reed-Farben. If I can help him get it he'll cut me in."

Martha looked angry; then a tired expression washed away the sternness. "Pete is a journalist," she said. "He's been on some good newspapers but he lost out. Whenever he gets . . . upset . . . he looks for a way to get back into the field. So you got the job?"

"Yes."

"You do it, and don't try to help Pete. You'll only hurt yourself and lose out the way . . . the way he does."

"He's got booze trouble?"

Her face hardened again for an instant; then her shoulders slumped. "Yes."

"Maybe if I do help him get a big story it will snap him out of it." Nick didn't believe that. You can promote a rummy to head of the firm and give him a ten-thousand-dollar bonus and he'll drink to celebrate. Fire him and he'll drink to ease his sorrow. They don't stop till they're ready or get the right kind of psychological help. But as Jim Perry, truckdriver, he permitted himself to offer the idea of a quick cure.

"You listen to *me*, Jim. You do your job at Reed-Farben and keep your nose out of all their other business. Now I mean this."

"What have they got to be so secret about?" Nick asked with all the innocence he could fake. "I've got security clearance, I'm not going to snoop for any government secrets, but if it's just a good story. . . ."

Martha's hand covered his for an instant. "Dear," she said softly, "don't you think I know what I'm talking about?"

"Sure. You've been around here a lot longer than I have."

"Reed-Farben is big business. Didn't you ever hear about industrial spying? Like a firm gets a great new product and they have to protect it? Well—this company protects, believe me. You keep out of it."

"They invent a way to grow artificial hair or reduce weight without dieting? Something like that would be worth millions."

Her eyes narrowed and he thought for an instant he had gone too far. When you were acting, dissembling, trying to pump and building a course of action all at the same time you walked a tightrope.

"Don't even think about what they might be doing," she ordered. "Did you see Kenny?"

"Yes. I just mentioned that you cashed my checks, and it was a breeze. They needed a driver. I found that out from the platform guy, Rainey. Know him?"

"He comes in. Promise me you'll forget about being nosy?"

"Sure. But is it all right if I go around with my eyes open? People will think I'm nuts if I keep 'em closed."

It got a chuckle. He liked the way it softened her lips and rounded her plump cheeks. Bob Half-Crow was signaling. Martha stood up. "I've got to get on the job. Good luck, Jim."

"I don't go to work till four tomorrow. See you about nine tonight."

"Okay," she whispered.

Nick had been too busy with his own scene to keep an eye on the now-jammed house. He felt eyes on him. He found them, halfway down the bar. They met his own and slid away.

They belonged to a man who was shorter and wider than most of the others. Hard, questioning eyes in an ugly face above a smashed nose. They belonged to King Kong, the man he had taken the Colt away from in Hubie's room at the Silver Cloud Hotel in Forge.

CHAPTER III

Nick's expression hardened, although unless you were close to him and watching the corners of his wide-set gray eyes and genial-looking mouth you wouldn't have noticed.

He thought—Mister Five By Five, the Beer Barrel Bucko! How did he find me, by coincidence or design? What's his angle? Is he sure he recognizes me from the scrap at old Forge Junction?

The brown hat and coat had been a fair disguise, considering the feeble wattage of the Silver Cloud's room lamp and the dim hallway. King Kong might be uncertain. Nick got up and sauntered to the enclosure near the front where Pete and a girl cashier were busy. When he reached the head of the short line Pete reached over, took the check and pushed back Nick's dollar bill. "On the house, ole buddy. See you tonight?"

"Yeah, thanks."

Nick strolled across the wide parking lot, turning his head just enough, every few seconds, to watch the door behind him. Before he reached his Ford King Kong popped out of the door, looked intently around. Nick turned quickly away and continued on to the car, his shoulderblades itching. He fumbled with the door, saw King Kong take a few steps in his direction. Nick turned and walked swiftly back toward the diner, passing the burly man with the blank stare one gives a complete stranger.

Joe Felix was confused. He had tried to drink a juke joint dry yesterday and his head throbbed, his eyes burned and he desperately needed the boilermaker he hadn't had time to

order inside. Nick's advance caused him to step aside a little.
The way the gray eyes looked right through him without a
trace of recognition upset him. Sure this was the guy! Or was
he? Brown hair curled up in front of a cap riding jauntily on
the back of a head was a lot different than a brown soft hat.
The guy in the room hadn't looked like a working stiff. Almost involuntarily Joe Felix mumbled, "Hey——"

Nick whirled, used his thickest drawl, "Yeah?"

"You—don' I know you?"

"Maybe. Ah don't place you, though."

"Didn't we——" Joe Felix swallowed and thought hard.
What in hell could he say now? Sure this must be the guy,
but he couldn't blast him right here. He licked his dry lips.
Geez, this working stiff didn't look quite like the guy, at that.
The one in the room didn't have any big silly square grin like
this jasper wore. Joe decided to be real detective smart.
"Didn't we meet each other coupla days ago in Forge?"

Nick shook his head. "Not me. I been on the road. Maybe
you mean my brother John? People are always mixing us
up." He'll never buy this corn, Nick thought.

Felix felt a flood of relief. So that was it. "Yeah," he said,
"now I remember his name was John. Was he over that
way?"

"Yeah, if I remember right. He was late for our poker
game."

"Where's John now?"

Nick pretended suspicion. "What you want him fer?"

"I—I owe him a coupla bucks."

"You can give it to me fer him."

"Aw, I'd rather see him myself. We got along good. Where
can I reach him?"

Nick tried to look like a smart country boy. "I don't
rightly know, mister. You tell me where you'll be and I'll tell
him to call you when he gits back."

"When'll that be?"

"Three, four days."

Joe Felix reached inside his coat. Nick tensed. The stocky
man produced a notebook and ballpoint pen, wrote down a
number and handed it to Nick. "He can call me there. You
tell him I got some money for him. What's your last name?"

"Perry," Nick said, and then frowned as if he was angry that it had slipped out. "What's your name?"

"Joe. You be sure and tell him everything is OK, and I can put him in the way of making a nice dollar."

"I'll do that," Nick answered, and went into the diner.

Joe Felix watched him, scratched his head, hit his solid skull above his right ear with a doubled fist like a man testing the contents of a keg, and decided he'd get that boilermaker down at Augie's. Not many people around Martha's knew him, but he shouldn't push his luck. He could ask about John Perry later when his brother was out of the way.

Nick waited patiently until he could get Pete in a quiet moment. He described the man who had just left, asked if Pete knew him. Pete said he had seen him once or twice but that was all. Martha didn't remember noticing the man.

Nick stood beside Bob Half-Crow where he watched the service and the cash count and asked his question. "Says his name is Joe."

Bob said softly, without taking his eyes off the operation, "Name's Joe Felix. Been around here seven, eight months. Does something for the big shots at Reed. Comes and goes. Don't work. Mean. Tough. Loses money shooting craps at Augie's. Gotta gun. He don't like you."

Nick blinked. "Thanks a lot, Bob. Custer coulda used you."

"I'd've led him right where he landed."

Nick chuckled and went out to his Ford. Joe Felix was not in sight. Nick raised the hood, checked out the ignition bridle carefully. He leaned against the car for a moment in the clear mountain sunlight, admiring the bluish tint of the nearest peak. You got the breaks and you got some bangs. Finding Hubie's tape and getting the job had been breaks; bumping into Joe Felix was a bang. There were two big questions. Was Felix looking for "John Perry" on his own, because he was part bulldog behind that oafish exterior, or had his employers at Reed-Farben put him on the trail of the man he had seen in Hubie's room? If he was on his own, the chances were he wouldn't report uncovering "John Perry's" trail. If he had been set on the search, he might report his progress because he needed some positive results. But there was a good chance he'd keep quiet for awhile, because he wanted to avenge the loss of his gun and his defeat in the hotel room, then report it as a victory.

Nick took out his handkerchief and polished the rearview mirror on the side of the car. You needed it as clean as possible on these mountain roads. The nagging question didn't resolve itself. Joe Felix was a danger, perhaps a deadly one. When Kenny or the others linked John and Jim Perry they'd see through the flimsy subterfuge at once.

Nick drove the Ford the twelve miles to Augie's roadhouse and found Joe Felix, who now felt better with whiskey and beer chasers in him, trying for a five points in the crap game.

Augie's game looked the same to Nick as it had years ago. It ran fifteen hours a day in the big back room, with protection from the locals. Joe made his point and a six point and drew down before he crapped out. Nick got a place and made small bets against the dice. In a little while Joe Felix spotted him, nodded and frowned. From time to time he glanced at Nick. He was puzzled and thinking hard.

While Nick was questioning Pete and Martha and Bob about Joe Felix, the stocky man had moved precisely as Nick guessed he would. He had headed for the nearest friendly ginmill, the place Bob said he frequented, Augie's. He went directly to the bar and downed two ryes with a beer chaser and then did something Nick had no way of knowing about.

He stepped into the phone booth and got through to Benn's private line by using a code number. Joe's ego badly needed a lift. although he told himself he was protecting his deal by reporting some results. After he heard Benn's accented *'allo* Joe said slowly, "I found a lead to him."

There was a pause, then the gutteral, precise comment, "Well done. His name?"

"John Perry."

Benn's hard eyes glittered while he thought, truth or lie? He knew of no Perrys in the area, although he would run a check. He wondered if the fool Felix had remembered that he had offered no name during his conversation about the Forge incident, and Benn had been careful not to ask Felix would have fumbled and lied more—it would have done no good. Of course Benn's own men had checked the clerk at the Silver Cloud and reported the name on the register, Henry Riegel, which meant nothing.

Benn said, "You are making progress. Are you now proceeding as suggested?"

"Yes. It will take a little time."

"But you anticipate no further trouble?"

"Naw. Cut and dried now."

Benn trusted no telephones. There were questions he wanted to ask, but they must wait. "Would you like some help?"

"Naw." Joe thought of the price Benn had named. He wasn't going to have any complications. "I can't talk any more now. I'll call." Joe hung up.

He returned to the bar and popped his shot and a beer into his mouth like a man eating peanuts. He wiped sweat from his upper lip. He had lied to Benn—but he would find Perry. He realized that in his haste he had forgotten to ask the brother his first name. No matter. These local post offices knew everybody. He would find him. The whiskies were taking hold. He felt better. He decided to have a fling at the crap table.

After Joe hung up Benn replaced his handset gently, pleased with the precision with which he could now manipulate his artificial hand. The eyes above the mask were as steady and cold as a pair of round ice cubes. He pressed a button. The man known as Robert Rick came through the side door.

Rick was gray haired and trim bodied, and carried himself erect. You expected him to make square corners and click his heels.

Benn said in German, "The man Felix found in the room is allegedly named John Perry. Felix is looking for him, but he is such a fool. Put guards on that diner and the stores. Find Perry."

"When we do . . . eliminate him?"

"Without fail. At once, if possible."

Rick relaxed, his tone suddenly gentle. "You are tense, old friend. Do you think he's one of those from AXE? Perhaps —*the* one—"

"He fits the description."

"Ach! We have set this up so carefully—and we are so near success. A few more weeks, or at most two months—"

"Weeks." Benn took a metal ballpoint pen between two of the tentacles on his metal hand and snapped it the way a man might break a toothpick. "We are almost ready to—ah—contribute great changes to mankind."

Rick's chuckle was grim, not at all that of a benefactor to humanity. "We'll get him, Martin, and if he is *the* one, so much the better. Do you think there is any chance they know about the Nebraska experiment?"

"I was sure they did not—up until now. We have such excellent connections in Washington. Perhaps we ought to get them away from here now. I don't think they know about Nebraska, but you know how clever this devil is. How many others are with him? They might find the Nebraska equipment. The warehouse near the missile complex would be safer than here. Let's send out what we have."

"It will be like putting some of our eggs in another basket."

"That's very good, Heinrich! Yes—some of our hatched eggs in another basket." The metal hand banged on the desk. "All right. As soon as the plane is available. Arrange it tomorrow. Meanwhile—cock the traps carefully for Perry."

"Don't worry, old friend—" Rick left.

Benn knocked his metal hand against the edge of the desk three times, raising it slowly and then bringing it down swiftly like the blade of a guillotine. That devil! That mysterious American who had cost him fortunes, wrecked his grandest plans, thwarted him in Indonesia, The Netherlands, Rhodesia. You were never sure just what he looked like, except that the frame was big and deadly and the brain agile. He changed his background roles like a chameleon. Logic and careful research indicated he was the AXEman, Nick Carter, but how could you be sure?

Benn was a ruthless man who thought he never knew fear. He had lived twenty lifetimes in one—but this devil haunted his dreams.

In the last year or so he had begun having bad dreams, all the same. He dreamed he set up more great plans, using his tremendous wealth and international web of ex-comrades. He

borrowed billions, bribed governments and was about to monopolize the real source of all money with an oil cartel and
another in nuclear power. Just when he was ready to throw
off the cloak and re-create the old order in all its glory, one
of his trusted aides suddenly shed a wig and other makeup
and said, "I'm from AXE. . . ."

Benn always awoke perspiring.

When they had captured the one in the plant he had hoped
—but no. After all their special treatments all they could get
out of him was that he was an FBI apprentice. Nimura and
von Dirksen thought that might be a hypnotic pre-set reflex.

Perry? The metal hand came down again.

Nick lost twenty-nine dollars. He didn't catch any of the
house mechanics operating, but there were a dozen devices
and methods you couldn't check without time and equipment.
He had once seen a table with microcircuits built into its
three-quarter-inch plywood base, and the variety of modern
shaped and edged dice was almost endless.

Joe Felix lost at least fifty dollars. His mind wasn't on the
action. He left the game at last and returned to the bar. He
wanted to speak to Perry again, but how should he begin?
The hard, doughy planes of his face contorted in concentration.

Nick saved him the trouble by joining him. "Hiyuh, Joe. I
did lousy. How'd you go?"

"Rotten. Drink?"

"Thanks. I'm busted. You wouldn't be interested in buyin'
a nice .45, would you?"

Felix gulped, choked on his cigarette. What the hell! Was
it a gag? Was it blind luck? After that sour run on the crap
table he ought to be due for something! "Maybe. I bin thinkin' about gettin' one."

"This is nice. An automatic."

"Army type?"

"Yeah."

Joe's spirits rose. "How much?"

Nick squinted, hoping he looked cunning. Joe thought, he
does look like the guy. Brother? Could it be— Nick said,

"They're gonna be worth more, with these gun laws an' all. How about a hunnert?"

"Aw, those old cannons ain't worth that. What kinda shape is it in?"

"Perfect."

Joe's heavy brows squeezed together. When perplexed he looked more like an ape than ever. If he could only see this guy with a soft brown hat on. He said, "Let's see it."

"I got it home."

"If it's perfect I'll go the hunnert."

Nick downed the drink. "Meet me a mile west. I got a Ford."

He led King Kong in his Mercury up the road Martha had shown him, but he stopped in a clearing below the lookout point. He didn't feel that he wanted to take Kong to the spot which, for him, had pleasant memories. He spun the Ford to a stop and was out, leaning on the door, when Joe stopped behind him and stuck his head out of the car. "Hey, whadza idea?"

"I got the gun hidden in a box in the woods. Come on."

Muttering to himself, Joe Felix got out of the Mercury. When he was fifteen feet from Nick, Nick said in an entirely different tone, one with snap and command in it, the words loud and clear, "Now stop right there, Joe."

Joe stopped and stared. Nick had pulled the cap down over his forehead for the first time since he had met Felix. That and the voice did it. Joe said, "Goddam! *You* are the guy from the room. That was baloney about your brother."

"Right," Nick replied. "Now let's you and I talk. Maybe we can do each other some good."

Joe scowled. Events were moving too fast for him. He had a small automatic in his hip pocket. If he could get it out and use it, here was his four thousand bucks plus on the hoof. Joe swung his arms slightly and studied the placid face of the man who leaned back on the Ford as if he were relaxing for a suntan. The eyes were very steady, the kind that had bothered Joe all his life. The eyes of men who did not feel guilt and weren't afraid. Not many cops had them—you learned to tell.

Nick read most of the thoughts behind those heavy brows.

He had not planned this—events had dictated the situation. He couldn't leave Joe Felix loose to break his cover and ruin all his groundwork for investigating Reed-Farben. He had drawn Felix after himself, intending to capture him and turn him over to an AXE detention team. The idea of coldly killing him had not entered Nick's mind. Killmaster, yes. Slaughterer, no.

Perhaps the booze gave Joe extra confidence. He went for his automatic. Before his hand closed firmly on it he was looking at Wilhelmina's shortened snout, in view and leveled so swiftly he couldn't remember seeing "Perry's" hand move. Joe brought his hand into sight again, empty, and stumbled back a step, away from that blue eye of doom. Joe did not lack animal courage, but this! He took another step backward. "Whaddar yah gonna do? What's yer angle?"

"Reed-Farben doesn't need you any more."

"Huh? Benn said—"

Joe stopped, flushed. He was confused, angry, unable to see the pattern. But he knew he shouldn't have mentioned Benn. He turned and ran.

For his bulk and condition Joe was fairly fast. Nick stayed behind him with long running strides. He hardly had to raise his voice. "Hold it, Joe. You want it in the back of the head?" Joe ran faster. "Or in a leg?" Joe reached the edge of the cliff with the wonderful view and turned right along the rim.

"Halt!" Nick barked. Should he knock the back of that solid skull? He hesitated—thinking of the long carry back to the cars. He'd rather take Felix conscious, able to move under his own power.

"Stop, you damn fool." Nick made it louder. "Nobody's going to hurt you."

He meant it. In spite of his threats, Nick hadn't the slightest intention of shooting a man in the back—or even in the leg from the back. Joe scooted out of the cleared area and into overgrowth, weeds and waist-high brush, following the dim path on the shale. Nick put on speed, made sure the Luger's safety was on, raised the gun. He held the blow, running four feet behind Felix. The man might tumble over the edge.

Without further moves from Nick, he did just that. One

moment he was racing past a jutting boulder, the next instant
he was gone, his moan lost in the scraping sounds of falling
rock and shale. Nick hurled himself away from the edge,
caught the boulder and hung on. "Damn, oh damn," he muttered.

Somewhere far below there sounded a nasty, dull *whump*.

Nick holstered Wilhelmina, crept along the edge until from
an overhang he could see Felix's body crumpled on outcrop
two hundred feet below. The ledge came out almost level.
Nick spent the next hour working his way along the cliff face
to reach the body. Broken neck and severe skull concussion.
Nick searched the pockets carefully, replaced everything,
took nothing. Two hours later he returned to his cabin at the
Alpine, made a complete report on tape, and hid it. Felix's
body might not be discovered for days. If someone remembered them together at Augie's, the chances of anyone from
that place talking was dim. Anyway, they had left in separate
cars.

The big problem would be Martha and Pete and Bob
Half-Crow. They would remember Nick's asking about Joe
Felix. That had been a bad move, but how could he foresee
what would happen? If the BCI asked them if they knew
anything about Joe, would they say that "Jim Perry" had
been asking about the man? Nick frowned. A lot of bridges
to cross when he came to them. If he was very lucky, Joe's
death would be listed as accidental or suicide, and that would
end it—except for what might go on in the minds of his new
friends at Martha's.

And in the mind of Mr. Marvin Benn. Felix had revealed,
when the name burst out, that he was working for Benn.
That meant Benn had a description of the man who had
searched the room at Forge. He hoped they were looking
for someone in a brown jacket and brown soft hat.

Mr. Marvin Benn. Chairman of the Board of Prostoglan-
dins Corporation, President of Reed-Farben and officer of
several other firms. The mysterious Mr. Benn, more of a
phantom than Howard Hughes. Nobody even had an old picture of Benn. In the foreign countries where Reed-Farben
had connections—Switzerland, Germany, Japan, France—
there was no trace at all of Marvin Benn. Try a tax subpoena

and you'd get a lawyer and accountant who had never met their client personally.

Mr. Benn, Nick thought, you're too good or too bad to be true.

Robert Rick—the suave, friendly executive of Reed-Farben—was asking Martha Wagner if she knew John Perry.

Rick was a good customer. He often brought in big groups. She gave him her pretty smile as she said, "No. Never heard that name. Let me ask the boys."

The keen-eyed, straight-spined Rick didn't suspect a thing. Martha was used to questions by local cops, credit investigators, BCI detectives, FBI men, security checkers, jealous husbands and angry women.

She left Rick and said the same thing to Pete and Bob Half-Crow, "If anybody asks you, you never heard the name Perry. Jim, John or anything else."

Both men nodded cheerfully and went on with their jobs.

She returned to the booth where Rick sat with two large-size men who looked like junior executives with muscles. "They don't know him," she reported with what seemed to be regret. "Would you like me to check some people tonight?"

"Please do," Rick replied. "I'd appreciate it very much."

When they left he pressed a folded ten into her hand, in addition to the one he left for the waitress. Martha telephoned Abe Phipps, asked him to tell no one Jim Perry lived there.

Abe was brief. "Gotcha, Martha."

He took the word to Nick. Rick and his pair arrived next, got a blank from Abe and went along. Thirty minutes later Martha's black Lincoln slid into a parking spot out of sight behind Abe's house. Abe stepped out the back door. "Jim's in thirty-four. Rick was here."

"Thanks, Abe."

"Law?"

"No, personal. And thanks."

"Any time."

Martha went along the back of the row of cabins and tapped on Nick's door. Once inside, she went right into his arms. When they separated Nick patted her shoulder. "For whatever has happened—thanks."

"I don't know what's happened," she said. "But Robert Rick and two of his men are looking for you."

"I don't know them."

"They asked for John Perry, but that's too close to Jim Perry for it to be anyone else. What have you done, Jim? Or —who are you?"

"*Who* am I?"

Martha took the lounge chair near the fan. "Yes, Jim, *who?*"

He stood beside her and gently stroked her hair without mussing a strand. "Just a rambling truckdriver who thinks a lot of you."

"I'd like to believe it." She sighed. "But I'm Martha, remember? The girl you said was smart enough to grab Lucky Ed's just before Reed-Farben opened up big. I've handled hustlers and operators since I was fourteen. You're good, Jim. I mean your act is good. But I can't buy it. Are you a tax man?"

"No," Nick said. This was the kind of lying he didn't like, conning someone you liked who deserved a straight answer. "I pay my own taxes, but I know that some multimillionaires who can afford smart lawyers and accountants pay less taxes than their maids do. No, darling—I couldn't be a tax man."

"All right, we'll skip that one. You're either law or you're outside it and on the run, or—"

"Or?"

"Or you're dangerous, somehow. I was fool enough to help you get into Reed-Farben, and they've discovered you're a threat. I like you a lot, Jim, but I don't want everything I've built up wrecked on account of you."

He got two cans of cool beer from his small plastic cold chest. She took one without smiling. "C'mon, Jim. I'm waiting."

"Baby, it's going to get worse. Joe Felix fell over the cliff up where we parked. He's dead."

Her eyes widened. "He worked for Benn and Rick. Bob Half-Crow told you he was a Reed man. You're getting in real deep."

"Will Bob tell anyone else I asked about him?"

"I've already warned Bob and Pete not to tell Rick or any others we have a Perry around. The way things are going we won't have him around long, but we won't finger him."

"Thanks. Maybe they won't find me for a few days."

"Are you mad? Didn't you hire out as Perry?"

"Yes. How about Abe? When they check here—"

Martha flushed. "I tipped him too. He'll cover unless it's big law looking for you."

"No, it will only be Rick and his boys." Nick leaned forward from his seat on the bed and kissed her, very gently. "Thanks, Martha. You're a girl any man can be proud of. You protect him first and then ask questions."

"I'm through asking because I'm not going to get any answers. Now how about you getting out of here? Don't go far, baby. Not so far we can't see each other, but far enough so that we both won't wind up in boiling oil. I think you carry trouble with you that we can't handle around here."

"I'm not leaving right away, sugarplum. You've helped cover me so I may last a couple of days before the wolves snap. I've got a hunch it may take Rick and Benn a while to check their own employee list. Isn't that the last place you'd think to find me?"

"My God, Jim! Are you trying to commit suicide?"

"I like life, baby."

"Then you've got an angle. Are you going to steal one of their truckloads?"

"Do you think that?"

"No—"

She stayed until almost five in the afternoon. The talk died away. She realized her arguments were useless. Snuggled with her on the bed, Nick felt relaxed; only when he thought about the situation he was in did he sense a tension and unease he had to hide from the girl. He had stumbled into the vortex of evil plans set awhirl by evil men and his new friends shared the danger with him. Of course he ought to get away now. Hubie Dumont ought to have gotten away while he had a chance. A number of other AXEmen had faced the same problem in the past. Some of them were now just respected names on an honored list.

Duty, he thought. Some men dig it and some men don't.

It was the biggest gamble he had ever taken. The game was balanced, like a crucial last out in a tenth inning—one break, one slip, one vagary of chance could pick the loser and make it time for lights out. When "John Perry" or "Jim Perry" was discovered, and discovered one of them would be, it would be for him like standing in a squash court when a basket of warm rattlesnakes was dropped from the ceiling.

While he was not sure what had happened to obscure his presence, he could guess. Not many people knew "Perry," and the most obvious ones—Martha, Pete, Bob Half-Crow, Abe Phipps—clammed up at once.

The methodical Robert Rick checked personnel records, and among the names was a Perry; Flo-Marie Perry, who drove seventy miles a day to her packing job. They checked her out. She came from a mountain ranch family whose right name was Perrine. She was illiterate except for such simplicities as big words on boxes and some street signs. "TV did it," her father told Rick's man bitterly. "I appreciate you thinkin' about movin' her up at the factory, but it's true. She ain't puttin' on. Flo-Marie kaint read."

Every family named Perry within a radius of 100 miles was checked out by Rick's teams, using the telephone directory and calls at post offices to find them. No "John Perry" suspects were found.

Nick's most important protection was the usual corporate red tape. The employee list that Rick checked was eight days old. The details about Jim Perry were in transit from personnel to payroll to computer, from where they would be printed out for the next employee list, scheduled for the tenth of each month.

While Benn and Rick and, by now, two dozen of their henchmen searched for Nick, he drove company trucks past their windowless offices not four hundred yards away.

Nick was "Jim" to everybody who didn't press him. When he had to use a last name he mumbled "Benny" and used a scrawl on receipts.

He discovered that most of the incoming loads for the main building were tankloads of milk, glucose, edible oils and syrups. They were spotted in the receiving dock, and white-coated workers from the building staff coupled up the plastic and rubber hoses which emptied the loads. The staff people couldn't or wouldn't talk to you. They'd sign in the load, say "Okay," and turn away.

One night Rainey insisted Nick join him for beers after work, and there was no way out of it. So he turned it to advantage by suggesting they buy a six-pack and drink the beer parked in the forest shade. Rainey approved—"Helluva lot cheaper."

After three cans each they went and got another package, because they were getting friendly and hadn't exhausted all topics. Rainey had declared he liked Nick's work and strict attention to business. Nick hinted that he was evading an alimony-hungry wife, and the older man became almost tearful with sympathy.

"If anybody comes lookin' for ole Jim Perry," Nick suggested, "please forget I'm alive."

"I already forgot," Rainey answered. "Now I see why you signed yourself Benny a coupla times."

Nick blinked. Never underestimate! He led the talk around to Reed-Farben.

Rainey was voluble. "Marijuana," he declared. "By God, they gotta gold mine. I'm growin' some. Lotsa the boys are. But this ain't a real good climate for it, and we got started late. Gettin' as high as a hundred bucks a pound."

Nick knew that the going price in Mexico was thirty dollars a pound for weed and trash-free grass, which usually sold for double that in the U.S. Where in these mountains would there be a high-priced market for pot?

"I'll have to start me a garden," Nick said. "That's a nice price. But won't the market die out? How much can Denver take? We'll have to ship it a thousand miles—to L.A., St. Louis, Chicago. . . ."

He let it hang. Rainey chortled. "Ship, hell. You just shoot it to the Army bases. All the kids coming back from Vietnam are on jays and they turn on plenty of the rest. The WACS love it. You take Fort Hood alone. Ten thousand users. They demand fat, clean jays. No junk. They pay. Say six joints per man per day at least to stay well-stoned. Talk about a market! That's just one base."

"Geez—if we get caught shipping it in. . . ."

"Who's gonna catch? The MP Battalion boys are the big dealers. I got real connections. The Army is chicken about it. Hell, they caught seven guys in the 518th Military Police and they practically beat the bust. I tell you, man, grass is a big, coming business!"

Nick puffed air from his cheeks. "An' you figure our outfit has the inside track?"

"What else? Oh, they're making artificial hearts or some-thin', but that's a coverup. I'll tell you what they're prob'ly really makin' in the big building. Acid. I bet they've invented a super LSD. I read the waybills. I've seen plenty of lysergic acid come in and ergotamine and tartrate and caffergote. You know 'em?"

"I know 'em."

Rainey nodded wisely in the dusk. "I knew the minute I saw yuh, Jim. Smart. Now lessee how we can make a buck outa this."

"We'll figure it out," Nick assured him. "And I see the first move."

"Whassat?"

"Put me on pickups and deliveries to the big building all you can. Sooner or later, I've gotta learn something that will give us an angle."

Rainey belted Nick on the shoulder. "Thas' my boy. I was gonna send you out on a Nebraska run next week, but they switched it to a quick airlift. Our plant over there is prob'ly their Chicago warehouse for the stuff."

Nick thought swiftly. Nebraska? There had been nothing in his AXE briefing about any Reed-Farben plant in Nebras-ka—an interesting state, considering that it was the HQ for more defense operations than most people realized. Nebraska is SAC center, CINC center and missile control HQ. The public information officers would like you to think that in case of war the President and Congress and general staff will go underground in Maryland or Virginia. Not so, Nick reflected. He said, "Hell, I didn't know we even had a plant there."

"Warehouse, really. Haven't shipped stuff over there for a coupla years, but I remembered. Then last week they planned a run and then canceled."

"Omaha? That's closest to Chi—"

"Naw. Nearer North Platte. Less than three hunnert miles. That's what makes it stupid to use air freight. They're shipping stuff up, all right."

"Trailer loads at the big building?"

"Yeah. But they'll use one of their own vans to move the stuff up to the airstrip now. The whitecoats'll handle it."

"I know North Platte. If I ever get up that way I'll sniff around the warehouse. Might dig up something. Is it right on Route 80?"

"Nah." Rainey snapped the tab off another beer. "Off 80 on 61. Wouldn' surprise me if they're cuttin' and packin' the stuff there."

Nick said, "We'll find out. There's a dollar in it somewhere for us."

He stretched and sighed, outwardly relaxing, inwardly recalling facts his trained mind stored in astonishing number and detail. He remembered visiting a fantastic city near the headwaters of the North Loup. The MI major escorting him through the building that would be AXE's command post in a national disaster had murmured, "Everything you see will be duplicated—deep under the ground."

The "warehouse" mentioned by Rainey would be thirty or forty miles from the most secret, most vital concentrated nerve center of the United States government. Of course its existence was known; you couldn't help it, with a complex which had employed tens of thousands of workers and had a stand-by staff of two regiments and a battalion of Marines.

He probed Rainey for more information but the supervisor had none. He was as eager as Nick to "get more dope," as he put it, in order to cut themselves in.

The next morning Kenny Abbott went to Benn's office. He liked chances to get next to the throne. Benn was jarringly abrupt. "What is it? You said important—"

"The police called. Joe Felix is dead. They think he fell or jumped off a cliff."

"Where?"

"On Jackass Peak. His car was parked there."

"Tell them we are sorry."

"They want to know if he was on any special assignment."

"No. He was off duty."

Kenny left. Why did that guy make him sweat under his collar?

Benn growled in his throat. Accident? Suicide? Bah! Felix had really gotten close to Perry.

To the world Marvin Benn (still called Martin by a few of the old comrades) presented a stoic front. But inside! Ah, he thought, if you could see inside. Why does my luck go so high and so low? Did AXE assign Nick Carter—I *think* he's the one, but even that could be another AXE trick—to me personally, forever?

My luck is so bad. Look at the Krupps! Even little Arndt draws a half million a year for life because the Führer of the Third Reich decreed it. And me—still in the battle, dealing with fools and losers.

He buzzed for Rick, who marched in promptly. "Perry," Benn rasped. "You know he killed Felix. Felix must have gotten close to him. Have you any leads?"

"A few. The men are following them like hounds. We'll get him soon."

"Stakeouts?"

"Everywhere."

Benn snapped another pen in two with his metal fingers. "If Felix could find him, he wasn't far away. I have the feeling he is under our noses. Perhaps laughing at us."

Along the road outside the windowless building rolled a big tractor-trailer rig, lettered neatly above its ICC data, *Reed-Farben Ltd.* At the wheel of the International tractor was Nick, wheeling a load to Colorado Springs.

CHAPTER IV

Nick enjoyed rolling the big rigs through the mountains. When you fed juice to the big diesel and felt the tractor take hold on the hard climbs, it was like having in your hands the reins of 500 horses. On the long, dangerous downhill swoops you watched your air and felt satisfaction at the comforting hiss and bite when you pressed the brake. You knew you were *doing* something.

He left the trailer at the C. & S. yard, dozed for four hours in the cab, and made his meet with George Stevens at a rural intersection near Fort Logan. George was a slim, absolutely dependable AXEman who worked out of the Chicago office. The fact that Hawk had detailed him to Nick as a courier-contact-backup man was an indication of how serious the chief considered the Reed-Farben case was.

George hopped into the cab, leaving his car half hidden from the two-lane road. Nick handed him his tapes as they exchanged brief greetings. "It's all on there, George. A real pail of worms, and I don't see any fat ones yet." He briefly recapped the events of the past week.

It was AXE procedure. If you're working with partners nearby they're entitled to know; you may be killed and tomorrow they'll have to pick up the threads. When Nick had finished, George said, "You're in a bind. They're liable to uncover Perry any minute and you'll get it in the back. Hubie vanished as if he'd dropped down an old mine shaft."

"Maybe he did. I think he went under that fence through the sucker hole. Let's hope he's alive somewhere in that main building."

"I guess—you'll be going in to look for him—"

"I would have, before now, but I wanted to learn what I could outside. When we know what they're doing in there we'll be closer to the answers. Rainey's dope angle doesn't make sense. Although maybe some of the help are operating on the side."

They were silent for a moment. Then George said slowly, "But the warehouse in Nebraska near CINC city does. That installation is so sensitive we're supposed to check if anyone buys maps of the area. They could be photographing or mapping. Maybe doing traffic counts and watching equipment move. Or setting up a sabotage plan—"

"Is Bill Rohde still at Chicago?"

"Yes," George answered.

"I suggest you meet him in North Platte. Find that Reed-Farben property and stake it out by leaving Bill there. When they fly that load over, I'll join Bill and we ought to get some idea of what they're doing. It will delay my penetration of the plant to have a look for Hubie, but our duty is clear. The orders were to protect CINC first and always."

"Will do." George gave him a firm handshake.

Nick picked up an empty company trailer at FKM Dispatch and made an airport meet. The load astonished him. It was crates of monkeys. He signed the receipts *Q. Benny* in a weird scrawl and studied the papers when he was alone in the cab. The shipment included apes, chimps, gibbons, guenons, grivets, macaques, capuchins, owl and spider monkeys. They were valuable laboratory animals. He was thoughtful as he thundered toward the mountains.

Even the gigantic sums spread so lavishly by the federal highway program haven't changed the fact that Colorado grades are steep. The rugged country is slashed and sliced, filled and bridged, but it's still up and down.

On the long, seemingly endless Lathrop Rise, Nick hugged the right lane and watched the flashing red lights of a stopped car grow larger. When his headlights reached it he saw a woman standing off the road, looking dejected.

A white handkerchief fluttered in the night from the radio aerial. Smart girl, he thought. Not much traffic tonight, but the troopers will get to you eventually. His mind automati-

cally catalogued the car—red Porsche coupe 912, probably a
'68. He passed it, a slow thundering giant lumbering past a
turtle, and then lifted his throttle foot and eased toward the
shoulder. Red Porsche coupe! They weren't too common, and
one was usually parked in the executive lot at the Reed-Farben main building.

He dropped to the ground and walked back. The woman
met him in the darkness, colored by the truck's running lights
and the Porsche's flashers.

"Hello," she said. A crisp voice with an accent. "Thank
you for stopping. My motor went dead on the hill."

Nick could see a slim body, a white linen suit. He said,
"I'm from Reed-Farben. You headed that way?"

"Yes, yes. I'm Greta Stoltz. How fortunate. But do you
think you can fix my car?"

Nick rubbed his chin. Probably he could, but he hadn't the
slightest intention of doing so. He recalled the AXE files.
Doctor Greta Stoltz, Ph.D. Researcher. Part of the inner circle!

He got his flashlight, opened the hood, pretended to exam-
ine the distributor, ignition bridle, carburetor. He got in and
turned over the engine briefly, got out and sniffed for flood-
ing. There was no smell of gas, although the gauge had read
half full. "Plugged gas line or defective fuel pump," he haz-
arded. "Want to ride with me? We can tell the first service
station to pick up your car. There's one a coupla miles up."

"Ya—yes. I think I will. But perhaps I'll come back with
the repairman."

Nick helped her up into the high cab, waited until he had
the rig laboring uphill again. "Maybe you'd better ride all the
way in with me. If they need a part for that Porsche, you'll
be stuck here till tomorrow. They'll probably have to send to
Denver—"

"You think so? Ach. Yes, I see—it is possible. A foreign
car part. All right. And thank you very much for stopping,
Mister—"

"Timmy Benny," Nick replied. "I hate to see a woman
stuck out on the highway in these times. You know—"

"Yes. I felt uneasy. So little traffic."

"So will you do me a very small favor?"

He could almost feel her stiffen. "What?"

"Well you see, we aren't supposed to stop for anything. Or anybody. Now if you'd just be careful not to tell anybody that I helped you, there'll be no chance of risking my job."

"But I am Doctor Stoltz. They will thank you—"

"The officials will thank me, but in my department they'll always remember that I broke a rule. We're very—well—you know how strict we are at Reed-Farben about rules. It won't do me any good in the long run."

She had a warm chuckle, deeply musical. "Oh—of course, Mr. Benny. I understand. I will not say a word." He stopped at a garage. She talked to a mechanic and climbed back in with Nick. The big tractor labored up the grades. At infrequent intervals a passenger car caught up with them and whipped ahead with a jaunty, flashing sway of its rear lights. Once in a while a car came down the highway, at higher speed, seeming to dive past the cab like a swallow with two yellow electric eyes. How do I handle this? Nick thought—I want to get next to her, but it's dangerous to open your approach without knowing something of a woman's character. You can turn her off you forever with the wrong gambit. That guy who suggested treating a duchess like a whore and vice versa didn't know many ladies of quality or hustlers.

He said, "You been with Reed-Farben long?"

"Yes. You mean you've never heard of me?" She realized how that sounded and laughed again—it was like a chuckle, from deep inside her, as if it rolled around her generous breasts before coming out.

Nick smiled in the darkness. Now that was an unusual thought. What had the file reported as her age? Forty-six? She was well preserved. From what he had seen of her, she was firm bodied, without an ounce of extra flesh, she moved gracefully and she was groomed to the tips of those brown-and-white shoes. "No. I'm sorry. There are so many people working there. I don't even know all the other drivers. You're a doctor. I suppose you're over in medical someplace. I've never had anything wrong with me."

"I'm not that kind of a doctor, although I've had a lot of courses in medicine and I guess I might be able to offer sensible treatment for most accidents or illnesses. I'm in research."

"Like—chemistry?"

"Like chemistry."

Nick sighed. "I had that in high school. I liked to make compounds. You'd think—I wonder if anybody ever put these materials together in quite this quantity in quite this way? What happened? Let's see exactly what happens now."

"Why Mr. Benny—you should have become a researcher. You described that . . . beautifully. It's the basis of research. Didn't you try to carry on?"

"No money. Had to go to work. But you know—at one time I had the elements memorized. Not with atomic weights, but the old way. It sure pleased my teachers." He laughed. "I'm sorry our table didn't have Californium. Symbol Cf. Atomic weight 246. Isn't that a great name? Californium."

"Where did you learn about it?" Greta was interested. She should get out more, she decided. Locked in the Reed-Farben pattern you forgot what interesting people there are in the world. What interesting—men.

"From *Time* magazine." He made his laugh slightly bitter. "What a way to get an education."

"It's a perfectly good way," Greta said warmly. "Read. Books are the storehouse of man's knowledge. And magazines keep you up to date. I think it's wonderful that you remember Californium. Couldn't you carry on your education?"

"On a trucker's schedule? Most of us move like gypsies."

"Ah—" It was a sound of regret.

The truck topped a rise and rolled on a tangent along the mountain's shoulder. Nick said, "I usually stop around here to cool the engine and have a cup of coffee. Like some? Or a drink?"

"Yes. If you'll let me buy."

"Best offer I've had today."

The Algiers was a neon-ribboned, large building set off the road in the little valley called Aster Park. Restaurant in front, counter service on the side, a big Western-motif room at the back for the cocktail crowd and Scotch set. Nick tooled the rig into the back of the big lot, led Greta in the rear door and found a booth. The room smelled of warm bodies, tobacco and booze. A five-piece combo was working with swing and bounce.

Greta agreed on a vodka martini after a delay discussing just a beer. "I've never been here," she said, looking around. "It's—it's *earthy*. But I like it."

"Aw c'mon," Nick objected. "You mean a good-looking woman like you, a doctor and all—doesn't get around much? Tell your husband to get with it."

"I don't have a husband."

"Then all the guys you work with are blind. Or do you give them the quick chill?" He studied her. "No, you wouldn't do that."

"There aren't many interesting men in my—my department. They are all married and live in the—the compound. It's a very tight community."

"I've noticed."

"So you see—I don't get around very much." She returned his salute with the glass. She took a good swallow. He liked that. Nick had a mild dislike for alcohol—you saw a lot of the damage it could do in his business—but he didn't like what he called silly sippers. You either drank or you didn't. When you sat and played with a drink, putting on a pretense so shallow it shrieked the lie, you were like a poker player bluffing against a lock hand.

They got along well. After three martinis, four dances and roast beef sandwiches ("I like that," Greta said when he ordered. "You're very European. Drink is better with food. It gentles it.")—they were Greta and Tim.

She didn't even raise an eyebrow when he ordered a fourth round—and The Algiers boasts that it serves "cocktails to match our mountains."

She felt sorry for Timmy Benny. A truly handsome young man. Well, I'm not *old,* she told herself. And I've seen more of life than any fifty of these local women added together. The Third Reich's defeat, the flight to Austria with Hashi Zeckdorf and the two boys, which had turned out to be a mistake. Their months as wondering folk, hiding, starving, stealing. Alvin killed by the policeman. She and Alvin had been lovers, although she had realized, over the years, what a juvenile relationship it had been. Then the period in Vienna, still hungry but studying, studying, studying. The first job with Petrochemexper, a grueling eight years living two lives while she earned her doctorate. There had been only six men in what she called her sex life. She kept careful track. Not enough, she sometimes reproached herself with a giggle. I'm not a cold woman, oh no, oh no! Sometimes her sleep was disturbed by thoughts of *him*. No particular him. Just friend, lover, husband, warm and protective man.

A man like this one, under different circumstances, she thought, watching Nick's handsome profile. Your own man. Never to be lonely again, never to wake in the night and think-think-think and want-want-want and know the slow whirling emptiness. She peeked at him again. A man any woman might be proud of. How sad that he had not been able to continue his education. Or how lucky! She might not have met him. Ach—come now, Greta, she reproved herself, such fantasies are for schoolgirls. Or are they?

She could tell he liked her. His quiet combination of respect and virile attention was delightful. What had he said? *I think that "doctor" sounds important, but Greta is beautiful.*

She would have been even more pleased if she had known what Nick was thinking, and his was the judgment of experience. She's an interesting woman. That silver-blond hair eliminates the gray, I suppose, but what a body! Those brisk blue eyes don't miss a thing. She has the kindness of the educated who have also been around—the type primitive politicians eliminate at once when they take power.

"It must be nice to be a real doctor," he said. "I mean—I keep thinking of you as a lovely woman and then I think gee-a-doctor-too. It's like saying this is Sophia Loren who also wins Nobel prizes."

That brought the deep, rich laugh again. "That's the nicest compliment I ever heard. Or should I be jealous of Sophia?"

"No, no. You—you come across, I mean, as all woman. Lovely. But then I remember that you're a lot more than that. Maybe it's because I've found that most beautiful women are a helluva lot less than they appear."

"You're a keen observer, Tim. I like that."

"Just what does a research doctor do? Keep looking for new medicines—like a cure for cancer?"

"I specialize in geriatrics. Of course that's a very complex field now. Once it meant the study of old age and its diseases; now it means the study of the young, where the diseases may begin."

"Like—transplant hearts and things?"

"Yes. Even grow new ones. After all, everything in nature grows. If you provide the right seed and nourishment you ought to be able to—cultivate any growth. Does that make sense?"

"Sure. New skin grows on a cut. But you must get bored around our labs. The stuff we ship is so standard. Although I suppose you'll come up with something new someday—like Doctor Salk."

Greta sat up straight. He thought she paled. "Tim! You asked me not to mention that you gave me a ride. Let's put that both ways. Don't ever mention that I even whispered to you about my—my job."

"Okay. Industrial secrets, huh? We're close to a break-through, as they say—"

"Forget it, please—"

"I forgot."

It took another vodka martini to relax her, and one more to make her cling to him tightly as they danced. He could tell she was enjoying herself and that she liked him. Did professional women build dream castles around virile truckdrivers?

When they left she walked slowly, but steadily. The martinis had blurred her speech and her eye, but not her concentration. Stout gal! Not all of them could carry that wet cargo.

He stopped the truck in a turnoff near Copperpot Valley, a giant parking lot used as a ski area in winter. He pulled way off the road, cut the brights and took her in his arms. She didn't resist at all. Her lips were pliant, and she gripped him hard. He felt her breath quicken. She caught his tongue in her lips, and a slim forefinger tickled one ear. Well, now, he thought—all that affection and noplace to go.

Affection? Greta was a pressure cooker, and he was her valve. She kissed like a puppy going over its new master, and then like an Athenian call girl trained in Istanbul and polished by a Port Said pimp. She fondled every part of him she could reach and his every response increased her ardor. She worked at love-making. Hell, he decided, as she tugged at his shorts, if she's as thorough as this in the lab she must be a great researcher.

She stopped what she was doing and he didn't move, hoping for more. "You like that?" she asked.

"One of my favorites." He bent and kissed the top of her head.

She was multidextrous. Her hands and body didn't stop when she talked. "You're a well-built man, Tim. You want to make love to me?" The martinis brought out her accent, but he had no trouble understanding her—none at all.

"Greta, baby," he replied softly. "I've been wanting nothing else for the last five minutes."

The cab seat was big, and so high you'd need a ladder to peek in. She began to wriggle out of the bra he had loosened. He helped her, then pushed himself upright. She stiffened. "What's the matter?"

"Watch," he unhooked the little curtains over the sleeper windows, moved his jacket along the ledge, tossed his waybill pad onto the floor. "Look. Up one flight. A whole bed!"

She laughed. It was an explosion of hot breath and alcohol, and not unpleasant. He started to lift her. "No," she protested. "You. Get up there. I show you."

She had him nude in a minute, not even leaving him his socks. A deft twist and her firm body flowed over him, silken flesh on a strong frame. Everywhere she touched him pinpricks of flame seemed to sparkle, hot and exciting.

Then it happened so fast he only had time for a pleased grunt. She was up, over and on him like a gymnast, a perfect connection without a wasted motion or false start. Her delighted, "Oh-oh," of satisfaction echoed his own.

He let his head fall back. And they said Japanese women knew how to treat a man! He wasn't quite used to this, but it sure beat necking for hours and losing your edge. He ought to do more, but—

He closed his eyes and sighed. If it's inevitable, relax and enjoy it.

Later, not long in time, but with each moment packed with

emotion, he repaid her attentions. She loved it. She told him so. Then—as if the burner had been turned off, she softened in the darkness and cried a little and tried to explain.

"Baby," he soothed, stroking her hair, "what could be more honest? My temperature was as high as yours the instant you kissed me. You enjoyed it? Okay. So remember it, forget it or look forward to next time."

She chuckled a little at that and said, "It's been a year, you see. I don't know any men except at the plant. And I'm afraid—I mean, I don't want any of them."

He was sure she was going to say *I'm afraid of them.* They shared a cigarette. He said, "Suppose I let you out at the phone box at this end of the valley? When there are no cars in sight. Good idea?"

"Yes. And—thank you very much, Tim Benny." When she spoke softly like that it was deep music. It pulled at you. Marlene Dietrich had the same effect.

"And as for thanks—I'm the one to give them, baby. You're the greatest. You needed me? I needed you." All true —in a way.

She stroked his hand. "I'm glad you stopped for me, Tim."

"Greta—I'd like to take you to dinner tomorrow night. We won't take any chances. We'll go far away."

"I—I'd like that—" She was weighing the odds. He won. "Where can we meet safely?"

"I hope your car is ready—"

"If it isn't, I can borrow one."

"Go to The Algiers. We won't stay there, just leave your car in the lot. I have a blue Ford sedan."

"All right. Okay!" She added the last as a happy exclamation.

He braked at the phone box. Their lips touched briefly but firmly and then she was gone. He rolled on and delivered the trailer at the main building docks, met and shepherded and waved off by one of the silent figures in a white smock.

Before returning to the Alpine he made one round trip past the plant on the highway, scowling at the giant oblong box of the main building, crouching in the blackness above its mantle of night lights. It was like a watching, waiting monster. What were they doing in there? Or what lived in there that consumed tons of glucose and high-priced edibles? Maybe they had their own King Kong. Or billions of lethal fleas?

He went to his cabin, made a shape in the bed with blankets and pillows and slept wrapped in a blanket in the shrubbery near his car. Perry lives, he thought as he permitted himself to drift into a catlike doze with his senses half alert. But probably not for long, unless he's very damn careful.

CHAPTER V

"Jim Perry" was still alive when the barrel-refinishing machines started their yammer-wham-bang and the highway roar increased as the morning shift roared past on their way to Reed-Farben. Nick inspected the scene carefully from his nest in the bushes, then slipped into his cabin and showered.

He drove to Martha's Diner, headed for the side entrance and was caught by Martha herself before he got in the door. She popped out and pulled him around to the rear and into the nook off the kitchen where the staff ate. "Jim—Jim, I don't know how you're still in one piece!" She leaned across the scarred but clean-scrubbed table. "Abe Phipps was watching for you last night. He called me when you came in and said you were sleeping out in the bushes so I thought I'd better not come over there."

"Not even to see if I had a blanket?"

"Abe Phipps said you did—" she flushed. "Be *serious*. Did you know they found Joe Felix's body?"

"No. I'll be serious after I get two poached and a side of ham. Coffee now."

She got up, placed the order with the man at the range and came back, carrying two coffees. "The police want to call it an accident, but a friend of mine doesn't think so and he's got a lot of influence. They'll be checking."

"Let 'em. I didn't even know the guy."

"Oh, no. He came here looking for you by accident and you asked us all about him because you thought he was your long-lost brother. Come on, Jim."

Nick grinned, wide-eyed. "Yeah, honey. It could be just like that."

"You'd better come right down to earth and be serious. And think about getting away from here. Robert Rick and his boys had some good reason for looking for you, too. And one of them has been keeping an eye on the place since yesterday. They take turns. Sometimes inside, sometimes parked up the road or in the lot."

"But they don't know me, sweetie."

"They've got a good description. They double-check every man who looks like you. 'Jim Perry? Jim Perry?' they ask. I don't see how you've kept out of their way this long. Some of them were back checking all the motels. Abe Phipps told me. How in the world are you managing to work there without getting caught?"

Nick wondered about that himself. "Looks like I'm not very well known. Just a nothing."

"You'd better be thankful. They play for keeps."

"Oh," Nick asked blandly, but his eyes were on her. "How do you know that?"

She reddened again. "I have friends. I hear things."

"I'll bet you do. Who told you that Felix's death might not have been an accident?"

"A very important man."

"Who?"

"I'd rather not say, Jim—forgive me—"

"Pearly Abbott?"

She put down her cup with a clank. "How—what makes you think—"

"Don't lie. If you don't want to tell me, just say so."

It was the right tactic. Martha sighed. "Yes, darling. Our noted ex-congressman—"

"He's got a piece of Reed-Farben? That's why Kenny has his nice spot and listens to you?"

He had pressed a little too hard. Her lovely red lips, which had been soft and concerned, firmed swiftly, like those of a mother who looks from the baby carriage to the vacuum cleaner salesman. "You ask a helluva lotta questions, Jim. Pearly is a friend of mine. Kenny is too. I don't know what this is all about. I don't really know who you are. But I do know you'd better get out of this bind *now*."

"Aw, sweetie, it's all a misunderstanding. By the way—" All or nothing, he decided. "I heard an old friend of mine was up this way but I haven't seen a trace of him. Red-headed kid. Chemical salesman. Real nice guy. Name is Hubie Dumont. You ever meet him?"

She was red no longer. She was pale, shaken, astonished. Her fingers pinched the zipper slide on her neat blue blouse. Her sleek head made side-to-side motions but they didn't mean no. "Hubie—" She swallowed. "You know Hubie?"

"Old buddy."

She drew a breath. "He stopped in a few times. I haven't seen him for days."

"Any idea where he went?"

She couldn't meet his gaze. "No," she replied.

He thought that was probably true and she didn't dare guess. The cook brought over his ham and eggs. He ate slowly, watching her without seeming to. She drank coffee, put out a cigarette that was still plenty of silly millimeters long, lit another almost at once. He tried to think of a way to draw her out without alarming her further.

Pete came through the swinging doors from the dining room and turned toward the nook. Banked sideways toward it, you might say. His face was puffy red over unfelt weariness, his eyes looked like a man watching tragedy while his mouth grinned. You could smell him before he reached the table. Nick guessed he had been up all night and was hitting his pace, fueled by Scotch or rye.

He said expansively, "Hiyuh, Jim boy . . . howzzit goin'?" He winked one eye at Nick. It was like the blink of a crying clown. "C'n I have the day off, Martha? I got one coming." He didn't wait for an answer. "I'll be back in the mornin'. I took fifty from cash. Put in a slip."

He had trouble turning around. He used the wall as a prop, like a ship maneuvering in a narrow harbor. Martha couldn't keep the sorrow out of her voice. "Where are you going? Do you want to ride down to Denver and back with me?"

Pete completed a full turn, gave his sister what was supposed to be a smile of thanks. "No thanks, Martha, I've got things to do." Pete straightened, seemed to take himself by the collar. "Think I'll have a cup of coffee."

He drew a cup and joined them in the booth. Nick decided Pete was pulling himself together for the day, believing with the mad self-confidence of the experienced heavy boozer that he'd be in fine shape after a couple of cups of coffee.

"Pete," Martha said, "you ought to have a day's rest. If you don't want to come to Denver why don't you go up to Pearly's pool and relax in the sun?"

"Maybe I'll do that," Pete answered. "Yep. Now, Martha —everythin' is set for the day. Bob has the menus all set, and all the mornin' help showed up. If Molly Rainey shows up you'll have an extra waitress for lunch."

"Thanks, Pete," Martha replied. She kept her eyes on the table.

Except for the slurring speech, Pete was very businesslike.

Nick said gently, "Pete—you sure keep things under control. Planning a day's operation for a place like this can't be as easy as it looks." From the corner of his eye he caught a sharp glance from Martha. Pete just nodded agreement.

Nick went on, "You have to figure help ahead—call up extras—"

Pete nodded. "Yes."

"You gotta make sure the meat deliveries come in. Even with a big freezer you can run out—"

Pete sighed at the thought of the responsibilities. "Yeah."

"It ain't easy when the rush is on and the orders are flying—"

"That's right." Pete agreed that he had burdens.

"Do you remember Hubie Dumont?"

"Yes, I wonder where—" Pete stopped. Looked at Nick by raising his whole head so that his eyes would focus. "Hubie —who?"

"I told him Hubie was in," Martha said disgustedly.

Pete's eyes narrowed until their bloodshot corners disappeared. "He came around," he said slowly. "Nice guy. Martha got to know him pretty good, didn't you, sweetie? Then *pft*. He went. I thought he shoulda said good-bye to me."

"Did he say what territory he was workin'?" Nick asked. "I'd sure like to see that ole boy."

"No—" Pete hesitated. Nick would have given plenty to know what he was thinking.

Bob Half-Crow came in from the front section. He ignored Pete and Nick, said to Martha, "Looks okay for the day. I'm goin' home for two hours. Otto is here. In a booth near the front door."

The big Indian left. Martha said softly, "Jim—Otto is one of Rick's men. Maybe they know your car by now—"

"I don't think so. If they knew that much, they'd be right on my neck."

She got up. "Will I—see you tonight?"

"No. I'll probably work late." He knew that wouldn't hold up. Pete had said that Molly Rainey was a waitress. Undoubtedly a relative of old Duke Rainey, the platform supervisor. If you knew women, you could figure that Martha just might use her to check on what hours he worked —"that new fella from St. Louis or someplace?"

And Molly would worm it out of Duke. Nick hoped to heaven Martha hadn't mentioned his last "name." If a customer like Otto asked a waitress like Molly if she ever heard of "Jim Perry," and Molly said, "Oh sure, he works under my Uncle Duke at Reed!"

When they were alone Nick asked Pete, "Going for that swim?"

"Think I will."

"Any chance of me getting a dip in that pool?"

"Sure. They don't check. Just park and ramble in. Bring your suit. Coupla cabañas to change in."

"Where is it?"

"Sickler Road. You turn off about a mile the other side of Aster Park. Gravel road through Beggar's Notch. Go in about two miles and you'll see the iron gates. Some layout."

"Take a nap up there, Pete. Maybe I'll wake you up."

Nick left, with Pete looking after him suspiciously. But no heavy drinker likes to be told to take a nap.

Moving with the watchful air of a cat inside a dog kennel, Nick parked in the Reed-Farben employee lot and found Duke Rainey in his glass-enclosed office at the end of the big shipping dock. Most of the trailers were gone and there were four other drivers on the mourner's bench.

Nick gave Rainey the waybills for the monkey shipments as soon as they were alone, commenting, "What do you think of those, Duke? Monks."

"That's easy," the older man muttered so that the men on the bench outside couldn't hear him. "They use 'em to test the stuff they're making. What's closer to a human than a monk? Labs use 'em all the time." He chuckled, riffled through his clipboard. "I'd like a look at 'em. Imagine a bunch of baboons on a trip! Stoned and sailing."

"I got another angle," Nick said, wondering where Rainey spent his time off. He didn't pick up his vernacular in Copperpot Valley or Forge. "Can you give me time off?"

"Sure. If you don't mind losing the money. I can't cover you on that. The damn computer matches truck moves against time slips. What's the angle?"

"I got next to Greta Stoltz."

Duke whistled. "Nice goin', Jim. I hadn't thought of that. Geez—a good-lookin' guy like you. If you can get into her pants we might be home free. Play it up."

Nick swallowed. That was pure Copperpot Valley talk. "Duke—don't mention my name around here. I mean—just Jim to the other drivers if it has to come out."

"You mean Greta doesn't know you work here?"

"No—she does. But with a connection like that Perry isn't going to be popular with the other bosses, get it?"

"Yeah," Rainey said very softly. "You're lining up a real inside track. Okay."

"And do you know a Molly Rainey?"

"Sure. My brother's kid."

"She ask about me?"

"How did you know that? Yeah, she said Martha just wondered if your credit is good."

"Martha knows damn well my credit is good. She just wanted to know when I'm working and if I'm making out all right."

"Seems to me Martha's the one you better tell to keep quiet about Perry."

"I did. She sprung me on Molly before she knew I had other angles. You know how women think."

"Yeah." Duke rubbed his chin, his gray eyebrows touching each other. "You want me to tell Molly to dummy up?"

"Is she that smart?"

"No." Duke shrugged. "She'd wonder why."

"Leave well enough alone. We'll have to trust to luck."

Nick picked up his swim suit and found Pearly Abbott's mountain home according to Pete's instructions. It was in a fifty-acre end of Aster Park, wedged between two peaks. There were thirty acres of flat land in beautiful meadow, another twenty you could farm with horses but a tractor would always be a danger because it might tip over on the sharp rises, and against the mountains the cliffs rose straight up.

The valley would never be dry. You could never make a living in it, either. The location was beautiful, the land was good, but the seasons were short and every fifth or sixth winter was rugged enough to wipe you out.

No winter would wipe Pearly Abbott out, but he didn't depend on hard work and nature. Now the fields were mowed, trim and smooth, just for the landscaping effect. White fences held four Appaloosa geldings.

The owner before Pearly had expanded the farmhouse to twelve rooms. Pearly had had it completely renovated and added a wing with ten more. The two barns had been refurbished and painted white, and there was a new eight-car garage and a big swimming pool with a line of cabañas along its side. A man in khakis was polishing a Cadillac in front of one garagestall.

Nick parked, nodded to him as if he were a regular customer, and walked swiftly along a curved gravel walk to the pool. Pete was alone in the sun, a pot of coffee and a bottle of Scotch on the table beside him.

"Hiyuh." He waved to Nick and then at the cabaña behind him. "Change in there."

Nick had a dip, toweled himself and joined Pete and accepted a drink. Pete looked neither better nor worse than he had earlier in the morning. He said, "I figured you'd show up. You're interested in what I said about Reed-Farben, eh?"

"Yep." Nick told the truth. "I sure am. And now that I'm getting a close look at the layout I can see what you mean. They maintain security like a locked steel box. I've delivered some loads to the big building and taken a couple out but you never get near the doors of the dock. The white-coats don't even say hello. Just hand you the papers or sign for the loads."

"I don't think many of 'em speak English."

"Has Pearly got a piece of the action?"

Pete paused with his hand in the air reaching for the bottle. He drew it back slowly. "Man, you catch on fast." He looked Nick up and down. Said thoughtfully, "You got some build on you, Jim. Where'd ya get those scars?"

"Mostly truck crackups. How about Pearly?"

"Yeah. You probably know more than you're tellin'. Sure, Pearly helped set the whole thing up. With somebody else's money, of course. Pearly don't believe in fronting with cash. His Washington connections are the sweetener. You see the war stuff going out. The specially wrapped shipments—the waterproof boxes."

"I've noticed 'em. If you get your story, isn't it liable to backfire? Maybe you uncover defense secrets. Maybe Pearly gets sore, and he and Benn or somebody puts the clamp on Martha's business. Things like that have happened."

Pete shrugged. "I'm a journalist." He said it as if he were convincing himself. "I'll know how far to go."

"How about Hubie Dumont? Do you think he was interested in Reed-Farben?"

"Sure. He wanted to sell 'em chemicals."

"Come on now. More than that."

"Well—" Pete finally got the bottle and poured. "Awright. Yes. He asked too many questions."

"Maybe—dangerous questions?"

"Not to me."

"How about Joe Felix and Hubie? Think they knew each other?"

Pete downed a third of a shot, pretending he didn't feel like swallowing the glassful. "Now—maybe you're asking too many questions, Jim."

"It might all be part of the story you're looking for."

Nick heard a car coming up the valley road. He lowered himself in his deck chair, pretending he wanted to get the sun on his face. Pete stood up and went to the edge of the patio. The car came into the parking lot.

"Who?" Nick asked softly.

"Kenny Abbott. Come up to get his orders from uncle."

"Pearly is in the house?"

"Sure. He stays here most of the time in the summer."

Nick said, "I better get going. Don't mention me to anybody, Pete."

It was too late. Kenny Abbott and a slim, eager-looking young man in junior executive's uniform—dark suit, white shirt, striped tie—bounced up onto the tile deck.

Kenny said, "Hello Pete." He saw Nick and stopped. "Hello—Perry, isn't it?" Unspoken was the comment: what the hell are you doing here?

"Hiyuh, Kenny. Hello, Bart," Pete said. "You know Jim Perry, I guess. I invited him up for a dip."

"I see. Hello, Perry. This is Bart Auchincloss. He's with us." Us, Nick decided, meant Reed-Farben.

He could read young Abbott's mind. When Kenny had a chance, he'd hint to Pete that maybe he shouldn't invite truckdrivers to enjoy Pearly's pool, even if his uncle had told Pete to bring anyone he wanted to. After all, there are limits.

A door banged on the house side of the pool. A big, portly man waved and came across the smooth patch of lawn. He wore a white sport shirt and tan slacks—specially made, Nick decided; even XL extra-large wouldn't fit him. Pearly Abbott must weigh 300 pounds. He had a broad, square face with a fixed, genial expression. A florid hiyuh-ole-buddy look, like the soft old men cast as senior husbands on television. It wouldn't do to confuse Pearly with them. He just wore the look.

He mounted the wide steps and gave everybody his swift, wide smile. Pete, stumbling a little on the words, introduced Nick. Nick's hand was enveloped by one as big as his own—but soft. "Haryuh, Jim? Always glad to meet Reed-Farben people. I helped bring that industry here. What we need most —good clean businesses to provide more jobs so people can stay in our glorious mountain country. I hope you like your

job and stay with the company a long time. Build a future.
Help build the company. Help build the country."

Nick was sure Pearly could go on for an hour without asking for a glass of water. He spoke in rich, stentorian tones
that carried, the words rolling round and smooth-sounding as
if each one got an individual push. When Pearly turned to
Kenny, Nick saw that the old man's hair was pure white all
over and cut long, in genuine congressional hippie style.

Kenny was not a tenth the politician. He said shortly,
"Perry drives trucks. Shirtcliff quit. He got a job with an air-
line and flew to Dallas this morning."

"Oh goddamn." Pearly spoke faster but with the same
audio power. "I wanted to fly over to Bartlett to see Max.
Can't you borrow one of Benn's pilots?"

"I tried. All busy."

Nick said, "You need a pilot? I have a license. Limited
commercial. Instrument rating. Twin engine too—"

Pearly turned like a ballet elephant. "Well now—"

Nick was pleased to see that Kenny stood with his mouth
open.

CHAPTER VI

The ex-congressman looked like a painting of "The Elder Statesman" as he stood with his head up regarding Nick . . . or one of the statues of a Roman politician in the Forum, or a young lawyer's fantasy of Cicero. Pearly said, "Well, now, Mistuh Perry, this is quite a welcome coincidence. We have a Cessna 172 at the company airdrome. Are you familiar with that ship?"

Nick put on his confident and pleasant look. "Very. It's a fine model. Service ceiling 13,100 feet. Four places plus luggage."

"Could you put yourself at our disposal for about four or five hours? Ah just want to go over to the little strip at Bartlett. Stop maybe twenty minutes and leave some things and get some. We'll be back by dinner time."

"It's my day off from truckdriving," Nick said.

Twenty minutes later they were in one of Pearly's Cadillacs, headed for the Reed-Farben flying strip. Pete just seemed added to the crowd. Along for the ride. It was, Nick realized later, a mistake, even if the small man didn't weigh very much. Kenny would not fly with them, he would return to the house with the car and pick them up later.

A lot of people made mistakes that hot summer morning. "Marvin Benn" and "Robert Rick" had already made theirs by not checking with Kenny Abbott to see if he had hired a "Jim Perry."

Robert Rick was conducting a methodical manhunt right over the top of his quarry.

Benn made another mistake by sending the pilot, Shirtcliff,

86

to Dallas to get him out of the way. Benn planned to kill Pearly Abbott very soon in the Cessna he loved to hop around in. But Benn had other plans for Shirtcliff. He was a good pilot and Benn would need pilots, several of them, very soon.

Pearly had brought it on himself, although Benn had intended to eliminate him anyway, by hinting that Joe Felix's accident was suspicious and he hoped there wouldn't be any more. "Such ruthless eliminations," he told Benn sonorously, "are bad publicity."

"There isn't any publicity," Benn had answered icily.

"But there might be—there might be. Ah was a ruthless young man in *mah* time, Marvin. But ah have mellowed. Now we have a wonderful thing going here. Let's keep it cool, shall we?"

"Of course," Benn had assured him. Cool. You will look better *cold* anyway, you accomplished thief. If you knew what the real plans of Reed-Farben are, I wonder what you would do? Rebel? Demand a cut?

Benn had told Pearly—and many others—that Reed-Farben was on the verge of a great medical breakthrough. A cure for cancer? Ah, better! Better, gentlemen. Competitors might eventually analyze and copy a cancer cure. There would be public pressure for it, right? We, he told them, are about to produce—grow is a better word—perfect artificial organs! There'll be no more waiting for a heart or kidney or cornea from a questionable cadaver. Reed-Farben is going to supply banks of them! Perfect ones!

All of it, of course, was a lie. Not a complete lie, but nevertheless a lie. Benn and Rick and the *real* insiders had lied to everybody. The real insiders were a tight group of dedicated men who had known each other, done business together and in many cases fought side by side in battle, over long, long years. The "outside insiders" were the hustlers and manipulators and multimillionaires who had put up most of the money for the project. Men like Stosis of Greece and Cowper of Texas. Men who could hammer a fortune out of circumstance and other men, but who stepped out of their class when they joined hands with Benn, Rick and company.

It was a day of mistakes . . . most of them by born mistake-makers. And one giant one . . . made by Nick Carter.

At the neat hangar he checked out the ship, reviewed the charts, chatted with the young man who was on duty at the field. Pearly and Kenny and Bart Auchincloss loaded several boxes from the Cadillac into the plane's luggage compartment. Nick asked for a weight estimate.

"About a hundred pounds," Bart replied. "Weather good. Winds minimal."

Nick gave the ship a long, easy run into an east wind and let it fly itself off. He gained plenty of drop space before he made two gentle 90-degree turns and headed for Squawpack Pass. The chart showed the pass to be 10,640 feet up, a gash in the range that separated the east-west slopes like a giant stockade. You could fly over in an hour or so.

The mountain range welcomed them suddenly. The sturdy Cessna headed through the first peaks like a fly cruising between book stacks in a library. Nick waggled the wheel a fraction of an inch. The controls moved easily but response was sluggish. He trimmed, changed angles, increased the throttle setting. She flew well but she didn't cooperate.

The jagged heights reached out at them like groping gray-black arms, greenish below at the tree lines, turning into shades of tan above on the rock ledges. He came in lower on Ralston Peak than he had estimated and S-turned to pass it. Bart handed around oxygen containers.

Nick said, "Mr. Abbott—you've been over this route before in this ship?"

"Sure. Three-four times with Shirtcliff. Anything wrong?"

Nick shook his head. He had flown in the Alleghenies enough to know the precious tips a mountain pilot needs. (Pass peaks upwind, avoiding their downdrafts. Cross ridges at gentle angles, not 90 degrees, so you can bank away without a full turn if you have to. Fly up mountainsides with the sun to use updrafts. Watch your ceilings, wind, weather and weight.) Make a mistake in the mountains in a small general aviation ship and you'll find yourself losing 2,000 feet a minute, about as safe as jumping off George Washington Bridge with an umbrella.

Abbott leaned forward to peer at the rugged world which

was gobbling them up. He filled his seat like a plum pudding jammed in a teacup. He said cheerily, "Don't worry, Perry. We're on the right course. That's Ralston. Squawpack Pass is ahead 'bout seven-eight miles."

The gash in the range that must be Squawpack Pass was ahead all right—and, Nick estimated, another 800 feet up!

Nick cross-checked his height, speeds, rpms, and almost nil rate of climb. He went over details in a lightning recap. He had flown plenty of Cessnas, including the 172. This one was behaving fine except for her failure to climb easily. They were over 10,000 feet, but they weren't adding anything.

"I'm not worried about our course," Nick said gently. "Did you ever go by Ralston so low before? We're looking up at it."

"No. You sure get a view this way."

They flew through a stretch of bumpy air. An updraft caught them and Nick thought for a moment their problems were over. The ship gained several hundred feet. He turned ten degrees and headed for the pass. Suddenly they lost the gained altitude—with a jolt.

Nick reset the trim. Ship okay. Safe route. There's variable somewhere! "Mr. Abbott," he asked, sharply and suddenly, "when you came over with Shirtcliff, how many of you were in the ship?"

"Huh? Just—the two of us."

"Nobody else? On any trip?"

"No."

"Did you carry much baggage? Like those cases we have with us?"

"Hmm. No—no, just a big briefcase."

Nick got it. The 172 is designed for four people plus 120 pounds of baggage; or you can put a child or a lightweight passenger on a jump seat in the luggage space, provided he doesn't weigh over 120 pounds and you don't carry luggage. There's a safety margin, the ship will do better—*but not in high mountains with downdrafts!*

Nick figured rapidly. The 120 pounds for baggage was taken up by Pearly's poundage alone! Bart had said "about a hundred pounds" when questioned about the cases he had piled in the luggage compartment. Come to think of it, Bart looked like a lad who had never carried a heavy box in his life—Mama did it all. Nick said, "Bart—how many cases did you put aboard?"

"Six."

"Did they *feel* heavy?"

"Well—not very."

That was ego talking. Nick remembered that the lad had been wrestling with the ones he had watched him carry. They weren't lightweights. He added. Call them forty pounds apiece. Hell and damnation!

He sat up straight, looking for a wide place between the peaks to turn, preferably in the nice, hot rays of the sun. There wasn't anything in sight that looked good. He eased as close to the portside cliffs as he dared, but suspected downdrafts. As it was he could see individual rocks in the shale and bluestone. There were a few places ahead, this side of Squawpack, which he could not see. Perhaps an escape canyon or pass he could put the ship out through or make a turn? He recalled the chart—not likely.

They were like an eagle that has flown into a sidehill mineshaft. No way to turn and a rock wall at the end. Unlike the eagle, they couldn't stop!

Nick switched the radio to emergency standby frequency, gave their identification and position, then said, "Mayday—Mayday—please stand by for a maybe Mayday. Will advise in a few minutes. Ask for standby for search at Richards-Gebaur Air Base."

"My God, is it that bad?" Pearly Abbott roared.

"What happened?" Bart peeped.

"Aw hell," muttered Pete.

"Sit tight, boys," Nick said. "We've got too much weight and a bad day for it."

"Let's throw stuff overboard," Pearly yelped.

"Shut up and sit still," Nick snapped. If they had time they could dump the cases—but the crags and outcrops were reaching for them now. With his extra-keen vision Nick could see details of the valley floor, a brutal mass of piñons, junipers and cedars, with some tall ponderosa pines shafting up like spears. Land in it and you wouldn't live for a hundred feet. They were passing a sheer slope of five hundred feet or more of brown-gray sandstone and rock with a few ledges in it like narrow steps. Try a landing on one of them? Suicide. The ship would carom off for a death drop.

"Oh my God," Pearly gasped. "You mean we can't turn back and we can't get over?"

Nick shot a glance at the three double chins leaning toward him. Pearly was pearl colored, the florid flush like a corpse with paint on the features. Nick felt guilty. It was his fault they were in this mess, even if Bart had made the major error. It was a pilot's job to double-check.

He gave Pearly a wide grin. "Just hang on, Mr. Abbott, and I'll show you a ride. Nothing to worry about."

Bart squeaked, "You can't turn. She'll fall off or stall."

"Shut up," Nick answered. "Put in your hours and get your ticket, and I'll listen to you."

Behind him Nick heard Pete say, "Leave him alone, Bart. He's a first-class pilot." Pete was lying to keep the lad quiet, and probably Pete didn't give a damn. This was as good a way to go as any, provided they hit hard and it was quick.

Nick didn't bother flipping frequencies to see if there was an acknowledgment of his Mayday alert. They weren't gaining a foot of altitude.

The ship entered sunlight. It was as if a powerful room light had been turned on. The sandstone cliff fell away and Nick carefully followed the curve of the mountain, studying the opposite wall—say 600 feet away?—with momentary glances—brief looks, because his eyes had to change focus to follow the near cliff. He was like a driver using a turn-out preparatory to a U-turn. Except that he had nothing underneath him but ultra-thin air, and the steering wheel didn't work very well.

He started the turn, riding the sunny wall and hoping for an updraft, feeling the weakness of his control as he tried to slew the ship around in a flat turn, yet use some angle in order to get around at all, and yet not stall—

The inside wingtip dipped and refused to come up at his touch, stayed sullenly down when he overcontrolled knowingly. He sat forward on his pelvic bones like a man on a jumping horse—you don't fly by the seat of your pants, you fly by the balance of your erect spine, but seat of the pants sounds more picturesque. They turned—slowly—ten degrees, fifteen. Then she lost her lift, skidded further over and dropped like a tired bird with suddenly folded wings.

Nick felt her with his fingertips. The well-balanced little ship seemed to say, "I don't want to do it—but there's nothing underneath my airfoils and cold air pushing down and in this thin stuff I've got to have speed to get lift." Nick took the long chance and let her fight for the speed.

They dove down the cliff face, angling out at a tangent that missed the steplike ledges by scant feet. Nick could feel her responding to his questioning fingers like a nervous woman, asking him when he was going to pull up, as if she didn't want to smash into the valley floor.

He let her go, let her lose gobs of precious height before he thought this is it and if she doesn't take they won't even find large pieces. He eased the column back, felt pressure and bite as she let him know with a dip of her tail and the lift of her new wing angle that she was fighting with him on his side. A rock outcrop reached toward them and he tilted the port wingtip up and over it and then they were headed for the valley bottom in a long, diving swoop with flying speed— if he could find room to use it.

She was sensitive again, responsive, partly from increased speed, a little from the lower-level air density, and some, he guessed, because by great luck he was heading upwind in the valley.

They were like a mosquito in a soup bowl. Nick took her down to the tips of the ponderosa pines, gaining all the extra speed he could, and flew across the uneven forest, studying the rim ahead and above. It was lower than the precipice they had just planed down, but his searching eyes found the lowest notch still at least 400 feet above their heads.

Everybody was babbling something. They had been talking or exclaiming all along but he had shut them out. Now Pearly's self-amplified question got to him. "I thought we had it. Are we going to get over?"

Nick gave him the grin again. "Of course. Relax. Enjoy this fancy flying."

Nick began the climb. Fifty-fifty chance, he thought, and

I've got to go over that notch at 90 degrees. If I angle in she may not make it. If I angle over she'll have to climb another 100 feet to clear the edges of the notch.

The engine hummed as if it could go on forever and this was a commuter hop from Stroudsburg to Teterboro. The tree line fell away but the brush-covered slopes were close and reaching up, up. Climb, baby, climb.

The lip of the rim was ahead—and above. They flew over blackoak brush and then the surface of the peak changed to windswept brown rock, polished by wind and rain and snow and time.

Behind them was a 1,500 foot drop, and beyond that another 2,000 feet to the next valley. Ahead was the course home and flying room and a slow letdown over the ridges and foothills.

Just ahead, over the rim.

Nick decided that they weren't going to get over. Not quite. What a lot of difference in life just thirty feet can make.

CHAPTER VII

When your reflexes are swift and your mind very fast, the real world seems to go by slowly. As they fought for those last feet of altitude that Nick knew they wouldn't get, real time seemed to stop.

Nick would be called a better-than-average pilot with a lot more experience than most amateurs, because the AXE vehicle and aircraft training schedule gave you a lot of time in varied equipment. But it wasn't really the AXE training that he called on now, it was the hours of fun flying that he and Mohawk Daniels had enjoyed, up on the edge of the Catskills near Kingston.

He recalled it all now, as the windswept rock reached for them. He never knew if what he *did* was an instinctive reflex. He thought he decided on it, but there really wasn't that much time. Instead of holding for the rim they weren't quite going to make, he eased back and let the rugged little ship flare a little—just the way you'd do when you wanted to roll-your-wheels-on-a-roof.

They lost forty or fifty feet, hit the upgrade of the rimrock and bounced once, twice, three times, like a ship trying to land in a cow pasture. They lost some speed but not much because the sturdy engine never changed its grind and the prop chewed doggedly at the thin air.

The ship bounced and rolled itself over the rim!

The world fell away suddenly for 2,000 feet. Nick got her nose down, talked to her. "Ah, baby, that was beautiful. Now take your time—get a grip—"

He didn't dare fuss with the trim. The Cessna lost 800 feet

and barely cleared the first ledge, and he eased her out. They were flying smoothly with nothing between them and the Kansas prairies but peaks and mountains that fell away like giant descending stairs.

Pearly choked, then found his voice—after perhaps the first time in his life he had ever lost it. "I thought we had it. Whatinhell went wrong? Perry—is the ship all right? You short of engine power, or what?"

Nick peeked behind him. Pete was staring moodily out the window. Bart was puking into his handkerchief. Nick activated the mike, canceled the Mayday. The air controller said sourly, "If you guys would file your plans with the Flight Service Station you'd live longer."

"You're absolutely right," Nick soothed him. "A lot of downdrafts today."

"A lot of 'em up there every day."

Nick grinned and looked at Pearly. "Too much weight— like I said. You're heavy, Mr. Abbott. When we weigh those cases we have on board I think they'll total a lot more than a hundred pounds."

Pearly looked over his shoulder at Bart. "You dumb son-uvabitch."

Bart was trying to clean his face. He didn't reply.

Nick put a call through to Kenny to bring the car. He landed the ship as smoothly as a woman setting down a cut-glass vase. While they waited for the car Pearly mopped his forehead and took Nick aside. "Perry, that was some flying. Not your fault about the overload. I heard Bart. We'll get rid of that boy. I'm used to 'em dumb but not that dumb."

"He probably hasn't done much lifting in his life," Nick offered.

"How'd you like to be my pilot? We can fix it up so you can get off the trucks when I need you or you can go on full time and fly company stuff when I'm not using my ship."

Nick had a hand-painted picture of Pearly calling Benn and saying, "I found a flyer working for us named Jim Perry. Gonna transfer him to the pilot list—"

He said, "I'd be proud to fly you around, Mr. Abbott—except—".

"Except what?"

"The super and the boys on the trucks are going to need me badly for the next few days, and I wouldn't want them to know I'm moving up. For several reasons. Now—if you could just not mention my switching jobs for about a week —till I let you know it's okay to make the move—"

Devious, Pearly thought. Perhaps a hustler. My kind of boy! And by God, how he can fly! He slapped Nick on the back. "We're gonna get along, Jim. You know when you work for me it ain't all work and no play, either. We have a little fun once in a while."

"Does anyone else use your Cessna?" Nick asked. "If not, I'll give myself a good check-out in her and give her a going over. I'm a pretty good mechanic on small stuff."

"By God, I did make myself a good deal," Pearly boomed. "Nope—nobody will use the ship but us. Where do I reach you in a hurry?"

Nick wrote the Alpine's number on a slip of paper. After it he put *Jim the Pilot,* hoping that Pearly might forget the name Perry. "Will you want to go up again today, Mr. Abbott?"

"Not by a damn sight. We were too near buzzard bait." When Kenny drove up, Pearly told him to put the cases in the car and deliver them. He didn't speak to Bart, who cringed into the front seat. They returned to Pearly's palace in silence.

Nick left Pete at the pool with a bottle and went back to the airstrip in his own car. The young man in the hangar office greeted him cheerfully and turned down the radio that was braying country music. "Gonna try it again?"

Nick grinned sheepishly. "You heard about it, huh?"

The man waved at a big receiver whose hiss was drowned out by the commercial station. "Standby. 'Bout all I got to do 'round here."

"Do you fly?"

"I'm learning. Slow. Got fifteen hours."

"I'm Pearly's new pilot. Gimme a coupla days to check out the ship and I'll give you some time."

The youngster beamed. "Great! I hafta drive all the way to Denver for a ship . . . and man, it costs."

"No small stuff flying out of here, huh?"

"Nah. There was a company Beechcraft in but the jockey wouldn't even talk to you. Same with the commercial boys. I never saw such a tightmouth bunch."

Nick gazed out over the raw, sunsplashed strip. A bulldozer growled in the distance, smoothing a shoulder of earth. "Not much action, eh?"

"Nah. I'm just a high-class watchman."

"Nuthin' fly out lately?"

"DC-3 came in last night and took off at dawn."

"Yeah?" Nick turned to his new friend with interest. "One of the old reliables. Carrying company men?"

"Naw. Cargo. Anyway, that's what they said."

"What did they load? Drugs and chemicals?"

"I dunno. They wouldn't give me a peek in her."

"By golly," Nick said reflectively. "I wonder where they'd fly a cargo that size?"

The younger man chuckled. "We ain't s'posed to know. But my brother works at air control. He took a look on the Air Force 'scope. They went up to Nebraska someplace."

Nick laughed. "Handy brother to have." He stretched. "Well—guess I'll make a call and do a little cross-country."

"Use the phone if it's local."

"It's long distance."

Nick went out to the booth and put through a short coded message to an unlisted Chicago number. All that was said by the girl on the other end was, "Yes, indeed." The "indeed" meant that his request for George Stevens and Bill Rohde to meet him at the North Platte post office would be forwarded immediately.

He flew the Cessna VFR down the mountains and was crossing the South Platte in less than thirty minutes. Sometimes you felt it was time to move, when a number of things lined up and pointed one way.

He met the two AXEmen, left his rented car in a lot, and George drove at high speed toward the northwest. As he tooled the superpowered AXE car along the highway which would approach CINC from the south he said, "The Reed-Farben warehouse is about as close as you can get to CINC without a security check. Bob Kline is watching it."

"What do they do there?" Nick asked.

"Nothing, it looks like. A car goes in or out of the gates about once a day. We can't even figure out who the watchman is yet."

"But there were deliveries this morning?"

"Yes. For the first time since we've watched. Two truckloads in an Avis renter. The truck was rented by a guy named Cowles, the same guy the car plates check back to. The address on the plate record is the Stockman's Hotel. He hasn't stayed there since he got 'em. We think he lives in the plant. He paid a cash deposit to get the truck."

They found Bob Kline sitting behind an abandoned barn with a view of a small, modern plant on the other side of the highway. It was well kept, the small lawn mowed. It might have been a little plastics specialty firm or a prosperous subcontractor.

"There it is," George told Nick. "Rented from the outfit that built it at a high rate by the Cowles guy, but they insisted on references and he used Reed-Farben and so we got the lead. He told them it's used for top secret testing or some such crap."

Nick said hello to Bob Kline, a serious-looking man whose gentle appearance hid a bulldog tenacity on a case, and a mind that explored every possible angle plus the impossible ones. Bob handed him binoculars. "They're doing something in there. First time the jalousies on this side have been opened."

Nick peered with the glasses through the screen of bushes. You could not see inside the building, and there was no close cover.

Nick sighed. So much for hunches. They might have to watch the building for weeks before a pattern built up, consisting of car licenses, long-distance photographs of anyone who went in or out, a further check on the mysterious Cowles.

"Well," Nick said, "I wanted to see it. I'm not sure why. Looks like I'd have done better penetrating the main setup."

He shook hands, exchanged a few friendly words, and he and George headed back toward town, leaving the other two on the stakeout. They had not reached Route 80 when the autoalarm on the car's receiver buzzed. George switched it up and Bob Kline's measured tones asked, "Mountaingoat Nine from Buck Three. Do you read me?"

"Mountaingoat Nine sitting by Buck Three Dot Two," George answered him in the responses that helped guard against trickery. "GA."

"Two top Army brass and a sergeant chauffeur just drove out. Headed north. Army limo. Three-star flag."

Nick sat up straight. Army brass *out* though none had gone in? Headed for CINC? He said calmly, "Turn around."

George spun the Mercury. "Catch 'em," Nick said. "Pour it on—"

The Mercury whined across the flat prairie road at 110 mph. Nick frowned. If that sergeant drove fast the Army car would reach the CINC gate before they caught up. There were several things he might do with the radio . . . there was also the possibility that the car and the brass were perfectly legitimate. Suppose the rented warehouse was an underground exit for CINC? Nick felt the warm sweat under his armpits. Nothing made sense.

He computed mentally. They should catch the other car in about forty minutes even if it was moving at 80 mph. What could they possibly do that called for a punch on the panic button?

If he could have seen the beautifully polished staff car pause at the first CINC gate he would have realized that the three occupants just might do plenty. The sentry in the gate-box was so busy standing stiff and saluting and unobtrusively poking the guardhouse button he hardly glanced at their pink plastic I.D. cards and pin-on signs that the sergeant-chauffeur handed out the window.

The duty sergeant who hopped across the road from the guard building took a better look. Lieutenant General Packard and Major General Burns, USAF, driven by Sergeant Swenson.

The duty sergeant stepped back and gave a nice salute.

The limousine rolled swiftly along the deserted, perfectly maintained boulevard leading into CINC. None of the three men in the car spoke. The two in the rear sat grim and straight, their heavily tanned faces and rugged jaws placid yet alert. The sergeant was efficient, driving with unusual precision. Indeed, the car and its occupants were too perfect. They might have been fashioned by painstaking model makers or TV prop and makeup men.

The car made the second turn to the right, followed a two-lane highway for a mile to one of the building complexes surrounded by another high fence. One of the cities within the city. This gate check was more thorough, although the same air of deference and subservience descended on the three M.P.'s on duty. The gleaming olive-toned car rolled through the barrier.

Looping through a miniature cloverleaf, the car stopped at the main entrance of a large two-story building on the edge of the city's airfield. It had the general appearance and atmosphere of a miniature Pentagon.

The two generals left the car and were passed through the main door and a security check at the elevators that led to the underground area—which was larger than the building above. At last they were in the office of Colonel Barringer M. Freestone, AUS, OD of PPI—(Officer of the Day—Plans and Position Indication).

Generals Packard and Burns extended their compliments to Colonel Freestone with the impeccable freemasonry of fellow ring knockers and union men. Freestone, uneasy about the funds diverted from the unbuilt SAC service hangar to the airstrip extension—no graft, you understand, just perversion of orders—was overly cordial. When they gave him the letters from CinC (Commander in Chief, quite different from CINC, which translates Command In Center), he stopped thinking. The letters were "personally signed."

If Freestone had lived he would automatically have looked up both generals in the Register, for personal and official reasons. It was a blessing, in a way, that Freestone, fourth generation Army and limited perception to match, never knew.

General Packard said: "The letter says general inspection, but I imagine the Chief was just saving words. We'll leave that part of it to AGO and GAO. What we really want a close look at are the PPI Intercontinental Thirty-Day Cycle files and operation."

Freestone swallowed. "General. . . ." He groped for

words. "Those are four-S files. Only General Sweet can show them. . . ."

"Of course," Packard agreed, with what might have been a tiny smile of approval. "Call him."

Freestone thought that he had never seen two generals who looked more like GS men than Packard and Burns. Steady eyes, square jaws, two hundred pounds, they looked a lot alike. Come to think of it, all GS officers sort of looked alike.

"General Sweet is away," he said sadly, knowing what was coming. "He flew to LA this A.M. Emergency meeting with Rand. He'll be back by five—"

General Packard looked less genial. "That's not quite procedure, is it? Technically—no one is in command with full authority—"

He let it hang. Freestone could feel it around his neck. "Well—this is a standby base. Hardly operational under normal conditions. We're ready to swing into active in a minute, of course, and General Sweet goes by the numbers, believe me—"

It was weak and he knew it. General Packard sighed. "I understand, Colonel. Not your problem, really. We'll take it up with him when we see him. I suppose you can give us a tour of command center, anyway."

"Certainly." Freestone made a small mistake and it was his last. Command center visitors, like viewers of four-S files, should have Recheck Security. He led his visitors to an elevator.

The cavernous command center room had a skeleton staff. Four enlisted men in the communication and control positions designed to hold forty, and one captain in the red seat in front of the two-hundred-foot-wide glass projection of the globe.

It was slaughter. The two tall generals shot Freestone first, the captain next and the four EMs in swift succession. Only two of them even left their chairs. The shots rumbled in the soundproof room.

Packard and Burns moved without speaking to each other. Burns to the silent elevator bank, where he noted that none of the three cars was moving and the one in which they had come down stood waiting for them.

Packard went to a low two-drawer file at the left hand of the captain sagging head down in the red seat. The file had double locks, with a tagged key in one. Packard carefully put a Magnum slug through the other, blowing it into the drawer. He opened the file.

He removed three files in red jackets, each not more than an inch thick, and a black plastic box about four inches high. The box had male plugs on its base, a great number of them. This little box contained the circuitry of several dozen TV sets, designed to perform a quite different function. If all the men who "knew" were dead or missing, this small box or its duplicate in Washington could continue to defend the continental U.S. and dispatch counter strikes.

Of course, analyzed backward by experts, it would reveal the details of the intricate mechanisms it commanded.

Packard wrapped the files and B-box ("Brainbox"—nickname for Autocommand Servo #725) in thin rubber coverings he took from inside his tunic. He and Burns went up in the elevator, got their caps from Freestone's office, retraced their steps through the long, almost deserted corridors and exchanged cordial salutes at the security check points.

The news was out. An M.P. captain was on deck at the main gate to give the distinguished visitors ("inspection—investigators" ran the comments on the internal phone lines) the sendoff they deserved. They returned his snappy salute with genial gestures.

The telephone in the gatehouse rang. A sentry answered it, gulped, stood up and yelled to the captain, "Sir—they say stop them!"

The captain yelled, "Halt," at the back of the car. It sped away as if no one in it had heard. He turned to the sentry. "Why? What did they say? Who called?"

"They stole something from control . . . they said." The sentry finished on an unbelieving note.

The captain ran to his jeep, raced after the big car without waiting for help. He had not yet fully accepted the situation. Those were two *generals*. The bosses.

The jeep could not quite catch the limousine on the long straightaway. They raced along wide open. George and Nick saw the two vehicles coming as they approached the base—their own car hurtling forward at top speed.

"Brake," Nick said. "Something funny here—"

Intuition again. This time it was dependable. "It's them," George snapped. "Army jeep trying to catch 'em."

"Wheel her around."

George jab-braked hard, got the Mercury down to sixty-five, made a looping turn on the prairie in a shower of dust and gravel, and gunned the superpowered engine as he turned into the skid. They were a poor third in the race, three hundred yards behind the jeep.

Captain Fownes, jamming the jeep's accelerator to the floor, was still wrestling with indecision. He had his pistol. Do you take a snap shot at two generals? If you were wrong, what a spectacular end to a career! He saw one of them peering at him through the rear window. Well—they knew he was behind them. He rapped out a series of dots on the horn. The old stop signal. He saw the rear window roll down. Hey —the guy had a pistol!

Captain Fownes' doubts were dispelled. He dragged out his weapon, realized he had no shell in the chamber, and the jeep's wheel fought him so vigorously he had difficulty pulling back the jacket. Finally he levered a shell into position. Almost at the same time a Magnum slug whipped across the jeep's hood, through the windshield and into his right chest. It was not a fatal wound, but the crash that followed was. The jeep twisted sideways and flipped along like a box tumbling down a hill.

The captain's knees, locked under the wheel, kept him in the vehicle for the first turn. The side of the car nearly cut him in two on the second go-round and then he was flung aside like a lifeless rabbit tossed away by an angry hound.

Nick and George gasped together as the jeep began its acrobatics. George took the Mercury off the road, fought its struggle to fishtail on the the uneven ground, braked lightly as he felt for balance.

"Don't stop," Nick said. "I saw gun flashes from the car ahead. I think they got that poor devil."

George did not reply, but the instant the Mercury settled he poured on the juice and got the car back on the road

again. They had lost another three hundred yards. "Think
you can catch 'em?" Nick asked.

"Ten bucks says we're faster," George replied.

"Bet," Nick agreed. He took Wilhelmina from under his
arm. They said it was an awkward weapon, even with a
shortened barrel and thin grips. He hefted the comforting
balance; in a spot like this, how wonderfully unawkward it
felt.

Nick saw the shadow before he heard the engine. He stuck
his head out of the Mercury. A blue Piper passed them
slowly and settled toward the big car ahead.

"Get this bit!" George growled. "These birds are thorough—"

"I wish I knew what in hell it's all about," Nick replied.
"I'm getting tired of guessing." What he meant was—am I
justified in knocking down that ship if I can?

"That's flying!" George exclaimed.

The Piper settled, flared until its speed matched the olive-
hued car. It paced the ground vehicle, flying a little to its
right.

The Mercury was gaining fast on the big car and the plane
that now paced it like a heron about to capture a trout. Nick
decided with satisfaction that he was going to lose ten bucks
to George. A coil of rope fell from the Piper. It had what
looked like a net basket on its end.

"I don't believe it," George rasped. "They can't pick those
guys up—"

"It might be done," Nick answered. "But that ship
wouldn't hold them. They're going to pass something up to
the plane."

George leaned forward, his big hands at quarter-after-nine
on the wheel. They were only three hundred feet from the
larger car. "Watch it. There's that gun!"

Nick leaned out his window, sighted, fired at the man looking back at them through the left side of the opening. Red
flashes spat at them. Nick fought for accuracy against the jolt
of the car, the wind pressure, the tears that dimmed his eyes.
It was worse than skeet on a windy day. Something *clonked*
against their car. The other man had scored first, although

Nick believed his first slugs had connected with the target somewhere. Nick aimed, followed, squeezed off—

The face and gun vanished. Hands reached out the window of the car and put something in the net basket. Nick made a decision. He would have liked to discuss it with George—a good man. But this was the kind of a spot they gave you the rating for. N3 raised the Luger and put his last three bullets into the cockpit of the Piper.

The pilot wound up his career on a note of pride. He had met the Army limousine exactly where and as ordered. He had dropped the net almost in their window, as good as in the old days when he flew trick runs like this for the movies. He felt no guilt. He knew his employers were crooked, probably some sort of spies. But they paid—

The sudden pain was terrible. He coughed, choked, let the column sag forward. The little ship fell off to the right, hit the ground with a explosive *crump* and pinwheeled over and over, shedding bits and pieces like a confetti bomb.

The limousine and the Mercury on its tail raced on. Nick inserted his extra clip. George knew the thought that was on both their minds. "They hadda be in on it. And we saw that Army guy shot."

"Let's hope it isn't just a runthrough for a TV program," Nick replied. "I'm going to try for their tires."

Another face appeared at the rear window, looking like the twin of the one they had seen before. It was oddly expressionless. You'd think in a situation like this men would show some emotion. Cool characters, Nick decided, as he squeezed off shots.

It took four. The man had just stuck what looked like a heavy caliber revolver through the window when the limousine lurched, began a side-to-side grotesque samba. George braked so hard the Mercury almost stood on her nose, with a shriek of hot scraping rubber. The car with the Army markings turned right and did a groundloop before skidding to a stop. The Mercury stopped sixty or seventy feet to its left.

Nick said, "Cover me."

He ran toward the cloud of dust that surrounded the other car, crouched, zigzagging. Fifteen feet from it he stopped, looking at the two men who stepped out and stood beside it like footmen. Beside the driver's door stood an erect sergeant, at his left a lieutenant general. They were of similar height, tanned, fine physical specimens. They looked as if they might be related. Both were impassive—their expressions a pair of blanks.

"Put up your hands," Nick barked.

Neither of them moved. Nick tensed. Another man might be hidden on the floor of the car. Suddenly he heard a tinny sounding voice over a carrier cackle. Did that general have a communications receiver in his hat? Nick caught the words, "Blow it—"

The general put his hand inside his tunic. The sergeant turned swiftly and put his head into the car and pushed or pulled something. Nick heard a hiss and a crackle. He turned, ran ten steps toward a small mound he had passed while approaching the car, noting it for possible shelter in a fire fight.

The first explosion roared before he reached the mound and he was blown the last five feet. The secondary blasts were spectacular. He opened his mouth to balance the pressure on his eardrums and crawled toward the Mercury. George had dropped flat. They both stayed down, heads sheltered in their arms, for nine or ten seconds.

Slowly Nick looked up, stunned and shaken. It took awhile for his eyes to focus. The olive-colored car was a mass of flames. Forty feet from it was a small mass of burning cloth that might be part of the general. The sergeant had vanished completely. Nick sniffed—gagged. Cordite, nitro, gasoline, flesh—

George staggered up beside him. "Geez—talk about guts—

"Or discipline. What in hell nationality were those guys? They all looked alike."

George shook his head, coughed, holding his neck. "Wow —if we hadn't hit the deck we'd have been hit by some of that junk. Did you see it go over us? Who were they? I dunno."

"We got under the blast," Nick said. He pictured again the faces of the men who had died so suddenly, so . . . *decisively*. They looked like the guys who modeled for outdoor clothes in the expensive catalogues. Like actors good at their roles. What kind of loyalty or training motivated them?

In the distance a siren wailed. "C'mon," Nick said. "Run me to the intersection and you can come back and help the Army and the local law check the details. Don't mention me. My cover is important now."

George whipped the Mercury back onto the highway—it had two small holes in its glass. "If those guys radioed a description of you you may not have any cover left," he said. "If one of them knew you—"

"It'll be exciting," Nick agreed. "But this bunch is just too damn dangerous and lively to let go of now. They're smart and deadly and well financed. I think you'll find they went into CINC and swiped something vital—"

"We better hope they did," George said as he let Nick out at the multilane road and spun the Mercury back the way they had come.

Nick wiped his face with his handkerchief as he walked slowly along. The white linen came away grimy. Great sense of humor, that George. Nick caught a ride with a Methodist minister who said, "You're the forty-seventh hitchhiker I've given a ride to this year. Sixty-one last year. My friends and family are making bets on when I get held up, or worse."

At North Platte Nick thanked him for the lift and sincerely wished him luck. The man had a kindly, speculative expression as he said, "Good luck to you. I guess I just want to see if I'm really a Christian."

The Cessna carried him back up the range into the face of the setting sun. She handled so easily he had plenty of time to think.

He was a few minutes late when he parked the Ford beside Greta's red Porsche in The Algiers' lot. He helped her into his car. She looked bright and active in a yellow dress that added to the scrubbed-blond look, accenting the silver-gray, immaculate hair. She gave him a vivacious smile and a warm hand. "It's nice to see you again—"

He took her to the Chez Rouge on the Denver road. It was supposed to be superior. He found the atmosphere and prices on a very high level.

Greta was cheerful and relaxed, like a girl from a strict boarding school on a night out in swinging surroundings. She held back, drinking the first vodka martini; the second went down easier and the third was half gone a minute after it arrived.

Nick sat very close to her in the pale blue light of the padded circular booth. "I met ex-Congressman Abbott. Interesting guy. He's one of your big investors or whatever they call 'em."

Greta tensed. "Yes," she said slowly. "He is—on the board of directors."

Nick leaned toward her as if imparting a deep confidence. "I got the idea Reed is on the verge of something big. I mean —real big. That ole boy isn't after peanuts."

"We are always—investigating," she replied, choosing the word carefully. "But—". She put her hand over his. "Please remember what I told you. Reed doesn't want—notoriety. Just do your job and keep your lips sealed and don't snoop."

"Who's snooping? What I'd like is a chance to make a little money. I've got a few bucks put away. If they're on the track of something hot you ought to jump on it too. You can bet the big shots like Pearly will be right in there. Why should they always scoop up the big gravy?"

She sighed. "You're right. But they are so—so strict." He was sure she might have said something like dangerous if she hadn't thought a moment. "If they thought we were even wondering about their developments—we'd be finished."

He thought the word finished came out too loud. "They won't find out if we keep absolutely quiet. The question is— what have they got on tap?"

"Well—you're right about its being big."

He snuggled lower in the booth, letting their bodies meet. He stroked her arm, letting it seem like absentminded affection. "Big enough to make fortunes for some people? Especially people like us?"

"Yes. You've been following the heart transplants?"
"Sure."

"The problem is the hearts. And kidneys and other organs, for that matter. The artificial ones are being improved all the time, but there's a better way that only Reed is exploring—"

"A better way?" he prodded very softly.

"Growing new ones."

"What an idea! Like you might—grow new skin?"

"Yes. In the lab. Grow it—them—ready for transplant."

"Millions," he murmured. "Billions. If they can monopolize it."

"They can."

"How soon—"

"I'm not sure. Actually—many of us aren't allowed into the main culture room." She laughed bitterly. "Imagine! Some of us think it's ridiculous, but what can you do? Anyway, only a select few see the end product. But I've seen enough. Done enough—"

"You helped perfect them? Greta darling, you deserve to profit! These big outfits always grab the money. Why should the people who supply the brains and do the work wind up on social security? Do you think they'll market them soon?"

"I think so." She toyed with her empty glass. "I grew the first heart in my section over six months ago."

"What a thrill that must have been," he said warmly. "To see your work succeed like that. Did you have to start with a model? I mean—do they still have to get—like—old hearts?"

"No, no. Just the pattern, you might say. The infinitely complicated particle chain. So that the computer can guide the growth steps."

"By God." He sounded impressed, and he was. "Step by step. I mean particle by particle—on orders from a computer—"

"Yes. People couldn't do it. I guess it would take a thousand people or more, watching day and night, to decipher and order the process. The way I—we—built it—it's automated."

"Wonderful. Wonderful! And once the programming is completed the process can go on. After the first one the production gets easy because the pattern is there."

She was pleased by his interest and enthusiasm. "Just start over. But you should see the first models of the cell structures. For just one segment—thousands of colored balls no bigger than pinheads on a wire framework as big as a desk. Nimura made the first one. He's a genius—" Mentioning Nimura brought her down to earth with a bump. She gripped Nick's hand. "You mustn't mention this to a soul. They are —extremely—secretive."

"Greedy, you mean. Don't worry, darling. The question is, how do we cut ourselves in?"

"I'll leave that to you. Stock, I suppose. But for both our sakes, don't—what is the phrase?—don't show our hand."

Or we'll get it chopped off, he thought. She evidently knew nothing of finance. Reed-Farben was a personally held operation; you couldn't buy a share over or under the counter. Lavish money from those mysterious Swiss accounts had launched the company, and the profits from the regular chemical and pharmaceutical production helped it roll. A good brain behind it. He wondered how far Marvin Benn would go in a legitimate operation. Not that Reed-Farben might not be legitimate—but a lot of the pieces of scenery were way out of place.

They had Chateaubriand and two bottles of rosé. Over the coffee and brandy, in a good moment, Nick asked, "Did you ever meet a friend of mind, Hubie Dumont?"

She laid her head back on the high padded rest. The answer came without hesitation. "Dumont? No. Never heard of him. Who is he? What does he do?"

"Chemical salesman. Thought you might have ordered something from his company—"

"No." Thoughtfully. "Drake handles purchasing. I just write an order. We are specifically discouraged from seeing any salesmen personally."

He believed her. There was something about Greta that persuaded you she didn't lie very often, if at all, although she could very cleverly if she had to. It began with little things, like the way she took honest gulps of her drinks, and her response to his kiss the night before. On a wider range, she hinted at a stoic philosophy . . . a realization that soon you will forget everything, and shortly after, everything will have forgotten you. She was a woman you would call *seasoned*, he decided, yet there was a freshness about her that said she had come through the mill without getting worn in the process. It was a shame she had wound up in these hills . . . on the

Washington circuit she would have been a hit and would probably have picked up a good husband in no time.

She looked at him dreamily. "What would you do if you made a lot of money and didn't have to drive a truck?"

"Take a vacation. How'd you like to go to Hawaii?"

She laughed and put her lips against his chin. It was then he looked up into the surprised and angry eyes of Martha Wagner.

Nick grinned weakly, started to say hello . . . but she walked on. She was alone. Oh, brother, he thought, it's not enough that I've got the whole Reed-Farben team hunting for me, now my best connection is going to be mad as a girl ignored can get—and that's mad. He said, "Excuse me a second, Greta," and followed Martha through the bar.

Martha's back was straight and stiff as she veered through the long room. She was searching for someone—at the bar, at the bar tables. Nick caught her two-thirds of the way to the far door, put a hand on her arm, said, "Martha—"

"Oh, leave me alone." She pulled the arm away, completed her inspection of the place, went out. Nick followed.

"Martha—are you looking for Pete?"

She stopped under the colored lights along the walk to the parking lot. She looked sad, angry, worried—and lovely. "How did you guess?" It was a cynical remark, not a question to be answered.

"I left him at Pearly's."

"I know. I heard all about your flying skill. And about your asking if Hubie knew Joe Felix. And your going to work for Pearly. You're going to get yourself ground up in the meat chopper, that's what you're going to do. What happens when Pearly tells Rick and the others he's hired you?"

"Are they still hanging around your place looking for— Jim Perry?"

She walked a few paces with her shoulders—usually carried with the squareness of a boy cadet—slumping in a tired, despondent slouch. "Why should I tell you anything?"

He walked with her. "Because we make a pair, Martha. We've both got worn edges."

"Is that what you told Greta Stoltz, too?"

"Come on now." He put an arm around her—very gently. "You can guess why I'm seeing Greta."

"Sure. Stirring up more of the same kind of trouble Pete is getting into."

"Oh. You mean Pete never took a drink till I taught him how—"

She looked up at him, the dark eyes moist and searching. Then she suddenly chuckled. A short sound, without much humor, a sardonic snort of realization and admission.

He matched it with a short laugh. It had a hard ring, too.

"All right, Jim," she said, not pulling away from his arm any longer. "I've been searching for Pete since seven. He often makes this one of his stops when he cuts loose. Yes— Rick's boys are still watching my place. I guess the big shots haven't tumbled to Jim Perry the truckdriver yet, although why in the world they haven't—"

"Somehow they've failed to ask Kenny about me."

"Or you're being led into a clever trap."

"Yes," he sighed. "Martha—go on back to your place. I'll take Greta home as soon as I can—politely—and meet you there. Maybe you'll get a line on Pete. If you don't, I'll help you look for him."

He kissed her in the semidarkness. She wondered if he knew how much she needed it—needed someone to carry a little of her load, if only for a while. "I'll be waiting," she whispered.

Returning through the bar, he wiped his lips carefully on his handkerchief.

When he stifled a small yawn Greta said, "You need some air away from this smoke and stuffiness," and pressed his hand.

After he paid the check and refused her money he said, strolling toward the car, "I suppose you put in a long day, Greta? Do they keep you on your feet a lot? Tired, honey?"

"The days are long. I do move around a lot. But I'm fine —" She guided him to the left side of the car. "I think you're tired. Let me drive. I love to try new cars."

She tucked him in and closed the door. He sighed—what angle could he use now? She maneuvered the car expertly through the lot and turned east, away from Copperpot Valley. Multiple martinis or not, she drove well, carefully, at moderate speeds, sitting erect with her hands spread properly on the wheel. He sighed, yawned again, leaned against her.

"That's it," she urged. "*You* had a hard day, eh?"

"A bone shaker," he said.

"Poor baby. You probably were very late getting through last night because of me. Just relax—"

She turned off the highway on a gravel road partway down John Reed Mountain, drove about a mile, and parked in an abandoned pasture near the small tumbling stream that probably had been the reason for the farm—long ago. There were no buildings left that he could see in the darkness. Gee, women were adaptable. Every gal in these mountains selected a private parking niche.

She wasn't like Martha, who responded on impulse, or—indeed—like many girls he had known. Greta was a methodical analyst used to coming to a conclusion—making a decision. She caressed him, fondled him, whispered to him, half undressed him, slavered in his ears, tickled his nipples with the tips of her nails, nibbled on his tongue—she came on strong.

Nick relaxed. Don't fight it, right? Be kind. Think of the girl's needs. People get enough disappointments in life. He shivered as she applied a special combination of touches. Wow! Admit it, Carter, this is good. He reached cheerfully for the Hudson Bay blanket he had in the back seat. Hawk would be proud of me now. Any sacrifice in the line of duty.

The uncut meadowgrass was an excellent cushion. In the starlight he watched Greta drape her dress on a sapling. Hawk would like this woman. Decisive, purposeful and neat. If he could introduce her to—

He had no more time for amiable conjecture. Greta kept him busy. It was as intriguing as it had been in the cab of the truck, only more so, with variations and room to turn. Greta knew what she wanted and precisely how she wanted it. He bumped back onto the grass after a particularly inspiring sensation. If Greta ever connected with the right man who could appreciate all this it would be a permanent connection.

The active and varied approach was stimulating, and you didn't run into it much any more. Maybe it was the fault of television; you sat on your can and absorbed two-dimensional pleasure and forgot how to use it for the real thing. This was enjoyable! Compare this girl to the unimaginative and flaccid types you ran into in Washington these days; the lazy ones, scared ones, green ones. Or, most boring of all, the narcissistic ones who lay like boneless mounds, rapt with their own fantasies.

Greta was a take-charge gal until she decided it was your turn to hold the reins, and it was good. She sure hadn't exhausted her skills in the truck!

"Turn," she urged, tugging gently at his bare hip. He turned.

It was novel, and ingenious. She breathed in his ear, many moments later. "You're a—hard man to get—and I'm glad—"

"It keeps the frosting on the cake longer," he murmured.

What a woman! He remembered the maxim about smart men preferring trained horses and trained women and grinned, glad she couldn't see him. That would only be true, he decided, if you had good stock to start with. You needed both brains and enthusiasm, because every skill depends on the intelligence you bring to it—

"Now," she said, "the way they say—sock it to me."

He stopped reflecting on pleasure to concentrate on it.

Later, when he lay looking up at the stars, she put a cigarette between his lips after leaving him to get it from the car. "Are you very tired?" She cuddled beside him. "You are very energetic, you know."

He captured a hand. "And you're creative, Greta. You must be a whiz in that lab."

He watched the stars, sprinkled across the purple like Christmas-tree sparkle snow. Why couldn't people just enjoy life, food, fun, sex? Which acted as a reminder. He had to stop this and get on with the job, find Pete. Still, there was time, all the approaches to that main building were bad, so the later he tried the better. And Greta might turn out to be a valuable contact. You could make believe it was in the line of duty. He pinched out his cigarette and turned and found her lips again.

At midnight he left her beside the red Porsche. She was understanding when he told her he had to get up at five

A.M., especially when he suggested they meet at the same time, same place, on Friday.

That made parting easy. Greta understood self-discipline. She had had no choice but to use it all her life. As she drove back to her little apartment in the Reed-Farben complex she thought over what Nick had said about making money. It was sensible, dangerous and very appealing. It would be very nice to have money and be free, with a man like Jim Perry.

Nick found Martha at the restaurant, in the private booth with Bob Half-Crow. A glance told him the answer—no sign of Pete. When the moment came, he asked quietly if they had any suggestions. Could he help?

Martha sighed. "We can patrol the joints again. He usually hangs around here a few days before he takes off for the big bright lights someplace. Then he finishes fast."

"Won't the owners of the other places call you if he shows up? Do you alert them?"

"They don't like me. Pete is a good spender."

It was answer enough. Nick said, "Tell me which way to go and I'll cover the road."

"Do you know Augie's and Deadwood's and Ferndale and—"

"Sure. And the Bar-Nuthin' and Jim Perrault's and Trace Quick's—I go west."

He was driving past the building when Bob Half-Crow burst out the side door, vaulted the iron rail as lightly as a deer hopping a fallen limb and stopped him. The Indian got in the car. "Got a call. Pete's just down the road near Wiggle Pass."

Nick gunned to the highway. "He okay?"

"No. Hurt."

The Ford could go. They covered four miles in 200 seconds, stopped where four cars were drawn up on the westbound shoulder. One of them was off the road, nose down, but showed little damage.

Another car had a spinning red dome light. A uniformed man was trying to use the radio, which crackled and spat. Nick and Bob ran to the car in the ditch. A man was holding a flashlight on Pete, who lay across the seat, moaning. He sat on the right, tilted to the left, as if he had not been driving. He was a battered, bloody wreck. If Nick hadn't known his size and skull shape and the jacket he wore that day he wouldn't have known it was Pete. A wheezing hiss of sound came from the torn lips, where the light caught a tooth hanging on the smears of red on his chin.

Nick said, "Watch him, Bob. I'll get a blanket. He'll go into shock."

The doors of Pete's car weren't even out of line. They lifted him out as gently as they could and wrapped him in the blanket on the grass. Pete tried to squirm as they moved him, said something that came out like a squeak and a gargle.

Nick bent low. "Easy, Pete. You're okay now. It's Jim."

" 'im? 'im?" The broken lips and battered jaw couldn't form the words. Nick held Pete's hand. It closed on his, weakly, just once.

"Yeah, Jim," Nick said soothingly. "You'll be all right now." He put his lips near Pete's ear. "Who did it?"

Saliva and blood spattered against Nick's cheek as he held his ear near the hurt man's lips. ". . . th' aching hen," Pete made the sounds with an effort. He wretched, spat vomit, repeated, " 'im?"

Nick squeezed the hand, whispered, "Yeah, Jim. Easy, boy. Who did it?"

". . . dey pekin hen." A pause, and Pete made a greater effort. ". . . dey makin' men."

A harsh voice above and behind Nick asked, "Whadda you guys think yore doin'? You shouldn' move him."

Nick stood up. The country law. Bob Half-Crow just looked at him in the car lights. Nick said, "He looked like he was going into shock. I got a blanket for him."

"Shouldna touched him. You know him?"

"His name is Pete Wagner. We're friends of his."

"Ambulance is comin'. I know his name. When did you see him last?"

Bob Half-Crow told him.

Nick tried to make it sound country-boy. "He didn't get banged up like that in the car."

"Naw, looks like he was mugged and robbed. Wallet's gone."

A stocky man in work clothes who had been keeping out of the way spoke up. "I know Pete. I saw him coming east and I gave him a toot-toot. There was a different guy driving and then in the mirror I saw the car U-turn. There was another car behind him. I'm pretty sure a guy got out and they went east in the other car. Anyway I was turning and I came back and found him—like this." He sounded sincere. "I called his sister."

Nick bent down suddenly over Pete's battered head. He felt for a neck vein, touched an eyelid tenderly as the cop said, "Hey. Leave him alone till the ambulance gets here."

Nick stood up and sighed. "They can check—but I don't think you'll need an ambulance."

Nick was right. Pete was dead. The aid men took his body and Nick and Bob helped the lawman make out his papers, then drove back to break the news to Martha. Bob Half-Crow headed for the kitchen. "You tell her."

Nick did, sitting in the rear booth, making it sound better than it was. She didn't wail or break up, she just took it on the chin and the dark eyes dampened—but hardened, too. Nick got up and brought them coffees and two shots of Jack Daniels. After some brief, sad words she was silent for a long time. Then, "You left him at Pearly's?"

"As I told you."

She went to the phone in the booth, came back in a minute. "He left there about five. Feeling no pain."

"I wish we'd got hold of him—"

"I saw you trying. At the Chez Rouge."

"That's not fair, honey. I'd have risked my neck for Pete, believe it or not."

She looked down. "Sorry. But I'm going to find out who did this to him."

"The law will."

"They can't find the men's room. And if they did you can buy 'em for the money in the coin boxes."

She was bitter. Nick thought of what she had said when the law came back—the man from the car and a BCI detective this time. They asked all the usual questions and no new ones. Nick kept quiet. Martha didn't mention Pearly, just told

them Pete had been on a bender. They nodded as if that settled it.

When they left she said, "See?"

"Not quite. They're overworked. You didn't help them all
you could. They might have used the lead that he left
Pearly's at five."

She sulked. Two well-dressed, happy lads bellied up to the
bar and Martha left him and went to them. Nick caught Bob
Half-Crow at the far end of the room, indicated the men
with Martha. "Know those?"

"Flash Waldo and Ben Milliken."

"They know Pete?"

"Sure."

"Drinking buddies?"

"Sometimes. They wouldn't hurt him."

Nick returned to the booth. Martha was starting right
away to try and get a lead on Pete's assailants.

When she returned he asked casually, "Any luck?"

"No. They just came from Forge Junction."

"Believe 'em?"

"I don't believe anybody."

"Think maybe he decided to get some personal interviews
for his Reed-Farben story—and they didn't like his questions?"

The dark eyes opened wide. He read anger—and fear. "I
don't—they wouldn't—"

"Of course not."

He had his answer. Not in the words; he didn't believe
them and he was sure she didn't either. He finished his coffee
and said, "I'm sorry, Martha. I guess you want to be alone.
I'll see you tomorrow."

He knew she didn't want to be alone. She wanted him to
help her avenge Pete. Her cool, "Thanks," hurt more than he
thought it could.

He drove to the Alpine, unlocked the trunk of the Ford,
carried three small cases into his cottage and drew the shades
tightly. As he put on black rubber-soled shoes and a dark
blue shirt the change was almost visible. Nicholas J. Hunting-

ton Carter, III, became Nick Carter, N3 of AXE, trained and equipped for his job. Jim Perry wasn't even in the room.

He lifted his shirt and buckled on what looked like a wide white nylon money belt. Its multitude of pockets held many of the creations of Eglinton and Stuart, heads of the AXE technical departments. There were tempered steel pries and picks and skeleton keys, shaped C4 explosives, lethal and paralyzing bombs, unbreakable bottles of sulphuric and picric acids—

In the cases were other belts for other ventures. The electronic one for trailing, with its beepers and sonic listener and radar detector; a wilderness survival rig, a straight combat assemblage, another with a recording unit and distance microphones.

Wilhelmina, the Luger with the shortened barrel and thin plastic grips, went into the form-fitting shoulder rig under his shirt. Hugo, the fine steel stiletto, was on his left forearm. He added a few items to his pockets and locked up the cases again in the trunk.

Before he turned out the lights he hung on his belt a neat case containing large size Pepitas—gas bombs with rapid expansion that incapicated briefly but did no permanent damage. Wilhelmina, Hugo, Pepita, Pierre, Lulubelle, he thought. The names had begun as quick codes for ordering weapons. "Send me a couple of Baby Swedes," sounded better if overheard than, "Send me two of the Swedish model submachine guns."

Like the Army, with their Long Toms and Honest Johns and Merry Harrys, the names were now standard for most lethal equipment. Perhaps they took a little of the sour flavor away from ugly-tasting business.

He headed west, away from Reed-Farben, and then took the road that circled the property to reach the airstrip. A mile this side of the strip he thrust the Ford between the clinging overgrowth of an old lumber road which he had spotted on his first day's wanderings. It became impassable in two hundred yards and he cut the lights. According to his map data and from what he had seen of the fences, he should be a half mile from the plant's rear barrier, where it angled behind the staff's houses on the plateau. It seemed like a logical place to penetrate. They couldn't be too careless with lethal traps, high voltage and those big-toothed Dobermans around families with children. The old lumber road gave out completely after a few steps, and he had to ease his way through tangles of hardhack and second growth conifers. It was a miserable jungle and hard going, but it also indicated that the guard staff might be overconfident about this approach. He nearly fell into the fence in the darkness.

He had already cut two sticks and sliced notches in the ends. Now he fitted a piece of wire into the slots and held the sticks with rubber gloves on his hands and grounded the fence. Nothing. It was the usual industrial barrier with triple-barbed wire on the top. He selected a low spot and used a flashlight briefly. One of the barbed wires was on insulators. Cut it and you'd drop a relay and close an alarm circuit. He dragged a sturdy fallen limb from the forest to the fence and propped it up. He cut the two strands of regular barbed wire, eased himself over the alarm wire and dropped inside the grounds.

Motionless he listened. All quiet. He tucked the minuscule receiver of his sonar-radar detector in his ear and listened. He heard both the carrier circuit crackle and the intermittent beat, but they sounded faint. He followed the fence slowly, toward the plant and to his left, listening carefully. The amplitude of the signals did not change. He made a shield, a web of wire, out of the piece he used to ground the fence and discovered that it would partially block signals from directly in front of him. The electronic watchdogs were not along the fence, they were farther in.

He crept over the brow of a hill and saw the lights of the plant buildings. The beeps and humming crackle in his ear were louder. He worked his way down the hill and, using the wire shield, located one source of the signals. A column disguised as an abandoned post from a rail fence. It gave when he tested it with his shoulder. He crouched like an NFL lineman and hit it. The post cracked and fell over, and he carried it several feet until the wires in its base were completely severed and he could feel clean ground between the ruptured post and the hole it had come out of.

Running swiftly, he sped across the hill at a slant, toward

the main building, racing past the production plants, on smoothly mowed ground now. He reached the little fenced compound that protected the power transformers and dropped behind it.

This was floodlighted area, and he squirmed until he was in the darkest patch of earth, prone at the base of the fenced square. Above him the powerpacks hummed softly.

A car shot up the hill from the gatehouse, its spotlight following the fence where it could reach it, spraying the grounds where it couldn't. A guard came out of the gatehouse—a tiny toy soldier at this distance—and took a Doberman from the kennel. He started off along the fence to the east. It would take him an hour to circle the property and reach the point where Nick had cut the barbed wires. There was always a chance he'd be so pooped by then he wouldn't notice them.

These moves, Nick decided, were just the first counteraction when an alarm came in. They must get them from time to time from animals hitting the circuits, and other accidents. A heavy bird picking up a grub from the grass could set off the sonar. But somewhere another crew must be working, wondering why the circuits had gone dead completely. If there was a clever oscillograph man on the power board tonight, they'd find the wrecked post in a minute; but the chances were against it. Fast, trained wire chiefs are almost a vanished breed.

When the car and the man with the dog were out of sight, Nick ran across the lawn and drive, vaulted onto the dock and crouched against the door of the main building, the one the white-coats used to reach the shipping platforms. With a key and a pry he opened it in seconds, slipped inside and closed it again. No alarm bells sounded. It was just possible the interior alarms were on the master circuit he had knocked out, or a main fuse had blown when he wrenched loose the post connections.

He was in a short hall of gleaming white facing tile. There were two glass windows at his left, the cubicles behind them dark. He went forward to where a main corridor crossed the hall like a T, left and right.

He peeked around the ceramic bullnose at the edge. What

a place to work! The long passages were like tunnels of glaring white ice, spotless and sanitary and nerve-tingling, as if you were in a cold tomb. There was a smell, a compound of all the operating rooms and dentists' offices and doctors' chambers the world over. Cloying, strong—laden with hints of steel-on-flesh and doom and death. Ether and paraldehyde, alcohol and lye, sulphur and petroleum, mankind's first and last aromas. Nick shivered. He liked to think he was emotionless when working, but this was something else.

Far to his left, toward what would be the office end of the building, a white figure like a specter on patrol crossed the hallway, probably from one office or room to another. Nick turned right as soon as the phantom was out of sight and went swiftly through the gleaming tunnel. He was almost black on white, impossible to hide and a wonderful target.

He passed offices, some with open doors, some with closed doors with names on them. All were dark. He saw laboratories as large as banquet halls; lights burned in some and there were sounds of humming pumps or small engines. Then he reached it. A double door of metal, which should open onto the building's center chamber, what had once been Lyman Electronics' production plant. The door glared with red warnings in four languages: DANGER. KEEP OUT. AUTHORIZED STAFF ONLY.

It had a good lock, worn by the insertion of many keys, many times. Nick went through it in less than thirty seconds, closed it behind him.

There was a barrier beyond the door, like those used in washrooms so that people cannot see in when the door is opened. Nick peeked around the barrier and breathed in. Emotion again. But who could contain it!

They were stacked and ranked like giant wine bottles in an aseptic operating room four floors high and long enough for a small-plane landing strip. No, not bottles, man-size test tubes, sloping gently outward, and in each one, regarding him with upside-down weirdness, was the naked body of a man!

The giant room was gently lighted, compared to the corridors, and Nick had entered on a third-level walkway. At intervals open iron stairways led up and down, and a webwork of catwalks crossed between the banks of coffinlike glass containers. He glanced up. A monorail track ran along the front of the high stacks; they could service them or remove them with some sort of rolling gantry crane. The room was absolutely silent. Those thousands of eyes made the hairs on his neck prickle. Automatically his hand found a pocket in the belt under his shirt, and he slipped on a head and face mask with large eye, nose and mouth holes. He carried a black one and a white one, compressed in packets no larger than a book of matches. For some reason he had selected the black one.

He went soundlessly on his rubber soles down the first shiplike stairway and approached the nearest ranks of men tilted in their grotesque test tubes. Then he saw the complex bundles of tubes and wires that ran behind the banks, like neatly bound, varicolored umbilical cords. He knelt down, peered between the glass cases. Every dormant body had a white tube leading to where a navel should be, a blue tube to the stomach, a red wire to the head, a green wire to the area of the heart.

He studied the nearest bodies, deciding that they tilted them down deliberately so that the eyelids would stay open. Was this mass murder, wholesale grave robbing? He swallowed, dismissed a quiver of emotion with trained will. To stand in the midst of so much death-life! He walked soundlessly past several pairs of upside-down eyes, and then he got it. As far as you could tell, every body was identical. They could be entirely synthetic!

He drew in his breath. Pete must have gotten this far, probably through that sucker invitation hole in the front fence. Because he knew the area, maybe he evaded the first guards and got through. They caught him, were going to run his car over a cliff to make it look like accidental death, but the driver had panicked when the stocky man blew his horn at Pete's car and braked because Pete wasn't driving it. Something like that—it made sense.

But *this* didn't make any sense! Unless—they had to grow the whole man and then they would cut out the needed organs from the synthetic prototype! Order your new heart— we'll slice it out of Number G999 for you (around the culture lab we call him Jerry Nine). Nick shivered again. The male bodies appeared to be complete in every detail. What about the ladies? "Sorry, ma'am, we don't stock breasts or cervixes."

What about that red wire to the head? Could these figures eventually achieve brainpower? Become thousands of better-looking Frankenstein monsters? Was Reed-Farben planning to market docile, ready-made labor slaves? "Buy your own help and exploit it forever—upkeep on glucose less than $1 a week!"

He studied the umbilical cords where they traveled along carrier hangers like sanitary wiring for a giant's telephone exchange. He followed them down the cavernous room, traced them through a wall where, massed together, they filled what must have been a double-door opening. He found a door in the wall marked KEEP CLOSED AT ALL TIMES. He slipped through it, crouched behind a waist-high closed tank.

This room, not as large as the one he had left, was near the receiving docks. Pipes led from built-in stainless steel tanks to the wall, and the umbilical cords, large white plastic pipes now as the individual tubes were joined, went out from the tanks. That answered the question of nourishment. He heard tiny whirs, clicks and humming sounds and crept along the tank line toward them.

A man in a white smock sat dozing, head in hands, at a U-shaped control console. It looked like a power or pipeline dispatcher's office, or a futuristic air controller's position. Beyond the panel, which glowed like city lights seen at night from a plane, two giant computers and their service accessory machines lined the wall. Tape memory units whirred. So much for the brain! But if they could program those artificial cultures as they wished—doctor, lawyer, Indian chief—soldier, politician, executive, thief—they had something *way out.*

A bell "tinged" softly in the console. The man in white lifted his head, read dials, pushed buttons, flipped a switch, glanced up at a clock . . . and put his head down again. 4:17 A.M., Nick noted. Time to be getting out of here, before daylight. Who knew what interesting traps this outfit had for those who got in past the barriers? They might have discovered the cut barbed wire by now. If Reed-Farben was just a business concern they sure played rough and for keeps.

He slipped through the door in the big room and closed it. He lightfooted along the "culture-coffin" racks, as he called them in his mind. He was six paces from the stairway he had come down when he sensed the silent rush from an avenue between the racks.

He started to whirl too late. He was grabbed from behind, gripped. Pinioned by a sweeping double-arm lock that almost immobilized him. The hard arms felt like steel bands padded with leather.

Before they completed their hold he was countering. He stamped toes, heel-kicked shins, grabbed testicles with a back-and-up twist of his right hand, sagged and twisted. He had never felt anything like it—powerful, implacable, frightening. The compressing arms tightened, hurt.

He shifted his weight, trying to choose a Nagewaza throw or Atemiwaza attack depending on his foe's response or counter. The trouble was—all the counters seemed perfect! Thumbs felt for nerves in his forearms.

Nick paused for an instant, although his mind worked faster than a bank of electronic relays. There was that smell of the operating room on the breath that whistled near his ear, countered him, paused with him, groped for nerve points with the skill of a top Judo technician. Nick, who had spent endless months on gym mats, practicing all the variations of combat which are lumped under the term Judo, recognized perfection. When he put himself out of Shizenhontai, or perfect balance, his opponent was willing to let him try the throw or hold, and Nick knew that he would promptly be topped with a better one based on his own choice!

Nick stood still. His assailant stood still too, one thumb nearing Nick's arm nerve, the grip rib-cracking. Nick pushed his 230 pounds sideways with a powerful leg drive—straight at the nearest row of glass containers in which the unseeing eyes of the dormant "men" faced the struggle.

The giant on his back lurched with him, then tugged him away from the giant test tubes. Nick lunged toward the racks again. It was the right tactic; his opponent didn't want them damaged. The arms around him released their lock, a hand fastened on his wrist, another tried to encircle the arm for a

Randori-Kata lock. Nick poked the latter one away with a short two-finger jab.

He took an overleg throw instead. He was hurled toward the far wall like the end child in a game of snap the whip. It looked a lot worse than it was because Nick let himself go, welcomed the break, let his foe believe in success. Nick, hands turned in and arms forming a hoop, rolled into the wall in a Zempo Ukemi breakfall. As he somersaulted sideways, his Hauchi—the "wingbeats" that cushion the contact and convert it into an outward or upward drive—were too fast for the eye to catch.

He spun to his feet eight paces from the one who threw him, balanced instantly in Hidarishizentai—perfect balance, left toe forward.

He faced one of the "men" from the big test tubes! A synthetic? This one seemed very "alive." He wore a white sleeveless shirt, white pants and low blue sneakers. The creature promptly assumed a Shizenhontai, perfect balance with feet even. Nick shifted to Migishizentai—right toe forward but absolutely central balance. The figure did not move.

But the contest wasn't over. Pale blue eyes looked into Nick's own like twin bulbs of cold, calculating, pulsing mercury tubes. Nick extended his right hand like a fighter coming out for the last round, wondering if he could deliver a Seoinage over-the-shoulder throw. The other's hand came forward a few inches, but not enough to cause kuzureta or disturbed balance, which would limit his options.

If they programmed these lads from that computer, Nick thought, they didn't miss much. He knew a Judo adept when he faced one.

Nick thought of Frankenstein again. He had his own monster now, the same squarish face without the grotesque scars. His monster was much better looking, like an expressionless, stoically murder-bent Mr. Clean. About 275 pounds of him, Nick estimated, and it looked like all bone and muscle.

CHAPTER VIII

A moving picture of what followed, on the black rubber mat amid the antiseptic-looking contents of the giant laboratory-production room, would be worth a fortune. It can never be duplicated. How would you organize two beings, one fighting for his life, the other fighting as if life didn't matter, and both with supreme technical skill in Judo, Karate, Savate and their dozens of subdivisions?

Every time Nick tried to escape or attack, the giant in white went into action. They fought Graeco-Roman, jiujitsu and American barroom.

For every attack there is a counter. For every counter a counter-counter. And for almost every counter-counter . . . well, you should read the writings of the famous Doctor Kano of Sodetsurikomigoshi fame.

Nick had no peer in Judo, even among AXE's instructors, where his abnormally keen eyesight, fine reflexes and constantly prime condition made him their equal. But this—

The creature attacked, defended, countered, blocked—to perfection. Once Nick was caught in the vicious Judo stranglehold (after a triple counter) Hadakajime. His lungs ached and he felt as if he had gone over Niagara Falls in a barrel after he broke that murderous lock—and he believed he might not have if he and George Stevens hadn't spent hours testing the *waza* extra-skill feat.

Nick's kicks at the groin were countered precisely with X arms. He used the X counter himself, carried it on with the hand-turned-in shin catch and was delighted to dump his opponent . . . only to barely escape a back flip and a rush for a

Katagurama. Nick countered, and nearly got a finger jab in the solar plexus and a neck chop.

He discovered that when he got a chance to assume the perfect balance position, his monster aped him, waiting for him to move. The creature could be immediately triggered by any attack or lowering of defense . . . and his counters and attacks were perfect and precise.

Swiftly Nick catalogued his weapons. Gas pellets and Hugo were out—he'd never have time to reach the first, and any perfectly trained Judoman can handle a knife attack. You may win, but you won't survive.

That left Wilhelmina, and he had a strong hunch this room and the others were guarded by alarm systems that would respond to any excessive noise. He thought—looks like I'm programmed for a loss.

Programmed? They were facing each other eyeball to eyeball.

"How'd you like to try something not in the program?" Nick asked.

No answer. Those cold blue eyes glowed and glittered.

Nick turned and ran.

He didn't dare look back. He dug in the rubber-on-rubber and fed every ounce of speed he could through his powerful leg muscles. He could do the dashes in near-record time—just hope they hadn't raised their boys to be record beaters!

He lowered his head and pumped his arms and he may very well have broken the record for the eighty yards between their combat area and the white tile wall near the control room. It grew near. He threatened to run right through it —or smash his skull to pulp by running into it.

You could figure these creatures were trained—programmed—taught—to pursue. And if they caught up, to tackle, strike and trip. It all depended on speed—they probably didn't program them too much about stopping. Anybody can stop.

Twelve feet from the wall. Nick huddled down, braked, twisted, hit it in the same Zempo Ukemi Hauchi—forward breakfall with wingbeats—he had used when the monster turned him into the other wall. He spun, thrust in reverse like a swimmer reversing at a pool wall.

The monster braked, slowed. Nick hit his legs at the knees, knocked up one ankle. The monster still had a lot of momentum when he crashed headfirst into the clifflike wall of tile.

Nick rolled away from the creature and lay panting. He had never felt quite so physically and mentally spent. The monster's head was twisted and punched down on his neck, as if he had dived into a pond with a stone bottom and no water. Little dying sounds came from the open mouth, and a red trickle leaked over the lips onto the rubber matting. The blue eyes hung half open. They had lost their glitter.

Nick put out a hand and took up two fingertips of the red fluid. Sniffed. It was blood, all right.

He got up and, puffing all the way, went swiftly out of the building the way he had entered.

Somebody had found something. All the ground lights were on. Three guard cars were parked near the hill over which he had come, splashing their spotlights around. The patrolman with the Doberman was coming over the hill, waving, and another was running up from the gatehouse leading two more dogs.

Nick trotted along the big building, behind the foundation shrubbery and circled to the highway side. As he turned east, around a corner, a giant figure blocked his way. Tall, 275 pounds, blue eyes—the monster!

Nick froze. He felt a spiritual chill. This was the man he had just seen die—or the creature he had seen extinguished? Square, mechanically handsome features, gleaming blue eyes, watchful as a Siamese cat taking a cold look at a new household puppy. But this wasn't the Mr. Clean monster, that one wore a dark jacket, pants and hat. Nick took a deep breath. Another one. One of the exterior patrols. Nick took a sideways step. The creature matched it, and said, "You come with me, please."

The voice was rich and musical, the diction perfect. It had the warm, mechanically heartless quality of a top-flight TV or radio commercial man, an announcer who has made good and gets residuals.

"What's your name?" Nick asked softly.

"John. Come with me, please."

"You ought to be called Frank Two. I met your buddy, Frank One."

"Come with me, please."

Nick drew Wilhelmina with a motion faster than most eyes could follow and held it close in. "Back up, John."

John came on, fading to his right, hand coming up. Another one, Nick thought, perfectly programmed for attacking all kinds of weapons. He shot John twice in the left kneecap, knowing full well the first slug hit the patella as accurately as the center of a target, but not sure if these creatures had sensitive kneepans. John fell like a tower with a dynamited base. The blue eyes rolled white. He could feel pain, all right.

Nick patted him for weapons, watching those deadly hands and feet. He found nothing and was not attacked. Perhaps a high pain stress short-circuited the brain on synthetics as it did on men.

Nick ran across the lawn, keeping shrubs between himself and the gatehouse. By the time a guard and dog came to investigate the shots, he was a tiny figure crawling down the bluff toward the gap in the chain fence near the highway.

Just before he went down completely out of sight of the plant and grounds, Nick looked back. The security force at Reed-Farben were having a busy dawn. He wondered if any of the men buzzing up the roads in the cars, following the dogs, climbing the hill where he had come in, and stringing out across the lawn as they followed his latest trail behind a Doberman, knew the inside story of what the company was making. Probably not. That's what the synthetic guards were for, to keep the interior of the big building sacrosanct. He took off his face mask, slid it into its pocket.

He crawled under the fence, left tracks and scent along the edge of the highway pointed toward Denver, then broadjumped with big, light strides across the highway and over flinty rocks into the woods. Running swiftly west through the overgrown meadows, he reached Bob Half-Crow's neat home in forty-two minutes. Nick tapped on the rear door. A dog barked inside, instantly silenced by Bob's strong tones. The big man opened the door—Nick had the feeling that a shotgun or rifle was within reach of one of those powerful hands.

Nick said, "I need a lift bad. About five miles, Bob."

In three seconds the Indian's black eyes seemed to evaluate Nick's black clothing, the cool, milky, sunless dawn and the empty highway. "Get in car," Bob said. "I'm coming."

Bob's Camaro was parked in the garage with the doors of the building left open. Nick found a piece of rope on a bench and tied one of his rubber shoes to it. When Bob came out and got into the car Nick held up the shoe. "I better drag this a mile. Lead the dogs away from your place. They'll think I tried to steal your car but the keys weren't in it."

"They know who you are?" Bob drove slowly out the drive. Nick dropped the shoe out of the door, dragging it on the ground.

"Nope. No idea, I don't think. Turn right, please."

"You lookin' for who killed Pete?"

"Yes." It was part of the answer, and true.

"If they have a real good tracker that shoe won't fool 'em. He can read what happened."

"It'll be the Doberman handlers and the local guards. Any of them good?"

"No."

Nick thanked Bob when they reached the lumber road.

The black eyes were expressionless as Half-Crow said, "Long as you help Martha or look for Pete's killer, I'll help. If you've got an angle that'll hurt Martha, we're all through."

"Martha is my friend," Nick answered, and went down the overgrown lane and retrieved his car.

At seven-twenty Nick rolled a big rig out of the plant and down the mountains. He dropped the trailer at the gantry yard, picked up an empty and met George Stevens on schedule near the Fort Logan intersection. Even if Reed-Farben had a spotter on him—and he watched for them—it looked harmless. You stopped for a drink of coffee out of your thermos and exchanged a few words with a tourist in the turnout.

This time the tourist had a companion, a slim, gray-haired man in a conservative blue suit who might have been George Stevens' successful uncle. It was Hawk, erect and alert, but from long association Nick spotted the concern of the extra wrinkles beside the keen, gentle eyes. Nick said briefly, "Hello, George. Welcome to the Rockies, sir."

As they admired the mountains—a casual group beside the road—he slipped into Hawk's hand the tape he had made at the motel recording the events of the past hours. Briefly, not looking at the men he talked to, he verbally summed up his actions. When his low-pitched narration stopped Hawk said, "Not much so far. Yet as potentially nasty a business as we've ever hit. Those last words of Pete's—do you think he was trying to say 'making men'?"

"Sure. Pete was a good reporter. He got the story . . . which he didn't live to file."

"George," Hawk said. "Please fill Nick in on what happened at CINC."

George outlined what the two generals had done, before he and Nick had ended their run. Nick gave a small sigh of relief. "I'm glad we didn't guess wrong. What did the coroner say?"

"There wasn't much left to look at. Maybe now that we know they were robots the autopsy will show something."

"I doubt it," Nick said. "These monsters are grown naturally. I think what's left will be flesh and blood. Can we tie in that grab at the CINC base with Reed-Farben?"

"Not tightly enough," Hawk said. "All we have to back us up right now is our story that the car came out of their warehouse."

"Look inside the building."

"We did. There are shipping containers and some bulk chemicals. The watchman has vanished. A call to their main office got us the advice that the Nebraska plant is inoperative."

"They've got us in the funhouse," Nick said sourly. "We don't know which door we dare open."

"We could go into that Colorado plant," Hawk reflected, "but if it's as clean as the Nebraska one we'd make no score and we'd be exposed. And Pearly Abbott would give us a few hot moments in Washington. Nick—are you willing to move on what Pete said? I won't tell you what to do, but you'll be gambling that he found something and that it's still there."

"I'm pretty sure of it."

"Then take the gloves off when you need to. They're not researchers benefiting mankind with artificial organs, they're criminals, no matter how damn fine their Dun and Bradstreet reads. But what are they going to do with those synthetic men?"

"I can think of a hundred angles," Nick answered. "Ninety-nine of 'em bad."

"I'd like a look at this Marvin Benn," Hawk said thoughtfully. "The way he stays out of sight is suspicious."

"Perfectly legal. An unseen personality like him is buying Nevada."

"Benn is clever. He has an arbitrage operation going that must make him or Reed-Farben a half million a year—"

"A what?"

"He buys and sells stocks, commodities, currencies, for a small sure profit because he has organized an efficient communication setup. It's a whole story in itself, Nick."

Nick whistled softly. "A man spread so wide—yet not thin. He's a genius. Which brings to mind—"

"Judas." Hawk nodded. He stood like a well-dressed tourist admiring the distant peaks. "We're looking."

Nick snorted. "With computers and seventeen major intelligence outfits . . . we can't trace that guy?"

"We can't even find the rent bills for our Saigon office," Hawk said with grim humor. "The Defense Intelligence Agency tells me they have over 500 linear feet of drawer space filled with unprocessed data. Somewhere in there is the item I want." He unwrapped a cigar. "You should read George Washington's detailed history, men. He had no money, few men, little cooperation and lots of treachery. He worked eighteen hours a day. His intelligence after the first year was excellent. He had a brain."

Nick and George kept quiet. When Hawk related examples from American history you listened carefully—after you discovered he was both inspiring and guiding you. "Violence," Hawk said. "It's the age. It's in the air. Watch 'em, Nick. I think their plans are big. Dangerous. Extraordinary. Greta may be your key. Are you going to see her tonight?"

"Plan to."

"Good." Hawk relaxed for a moment, his eyes twinkling. "Martha may be more interesting, but it's Greta for information. This life is hard on our personal tastes."

They discussed Pearly Abbott's latest gambits, including his unseen leverage on the Federal Highway Bill and the rapid expansion of the construction outfits in which he was an unseen partner. None of them brought up the raw question—how deep is Pearly in Reed-Farben? They gave him the benefit of the doubt until caught.

Nick wheeled the rig back up into the mountains. By five o'clock he had showered and was at Martha's—ready for a steak. Bob Half-Crow came to the booth the instant Nick sat down. "Jim. Martha's disappeared."

Nick looked up with an expression as unreadable as the Indian's. "When? What happened?"

"Nothing happened. She came in about nine and said she'd be gone for a couple of hours but be back for the lunch crowd. Nobody has seen her since."

"The car?"

"Gone."

"Maybe she just got fed up to here." Nick held a finger horizontally across his nose. "And she's taking a day or two off."

The black eyes narrowed slightly. "You know Martha. I know her better. She don't do things like that."

"Any ideas?"

"That guy Rick has been around an awful lot and he ain't looked happy. And I ain't seen him all day today."

Bob turned and walked away, like a man who has said it all. Nick's club steak was tender, perfectly cooked. He ate it, but he didn't enjoy it. At the agreed-on time—6:10—he called the number Greta had given him. Another woman answered, asked who was calling. Nick used the name they had agreed on, William Deutsch. Greta came on in a moment. "Hello. I'm so glad to hear from you."

"Like to do a little bowling? Usual place—about eight?"

"Yes. Yes. Thank you." She hung up.

Nick replaced the instrument gently. Greta had sounded—odd. She had kept the conversation very short. You might say she sounded—fearful.

When she parked the red Porsche and climbed into the Ford he saw at once that she was scared. Driving toward the secluded parking place, he asked her to light him a cigarette, and out of the corner of his eye he saw her hands trembling. Scared? Terrified. You didn't shake up Greta Stoltz easily, either. He said, "Tell me about it, baby."

Her voice caught in her throat. "What? What did you—say?"

"Tell me about what's happened," he urged soothingly. "Somebody has put you over the jumps today."

She gripped his arm and leaned against him. He found the familiar opening in the trees and backed the car in, cut the lights, kissed her gently. "Relax, darling. I won't let anybody hurt you."

"You don't know *them*," she said, and every word carried a weight of full despair. "They are such—"

"Monsters?"

She stiffened and gave a gasp. "Why did you say that?"

"A lot of big operators become monsters. For them there are no other people in the world."

"Ja," she replied. "How well you say it. They are monsters."

"Who especially? Benn? Rick? Nimura?"

"Nimura sees only the work. But those other two—ech!" Then it came in a stream, as if a relief valve had been opened. "My darling, our ideas for making money on Reed-Farben developments were so foolish. I knew we had made breakthroughs. They told me we could grow artificial hearts and organs. I saw them. Today I saw something else. We grow the entire artificial man—and then cut out the organs. That's where the ones I saw came from, but it is not the business they plan. Today Rick showed me a man—I mean a real man—on whom they are experimenting. I had to start a project on him. A graft of synthetic tissue to see how it can be made to last longer. Rick told me that the artificial organs are all right when implanted in humans and monkeys, but the complete men they grow die in ten or twelve days after they are removed from their tanks, unless they are connected to the umbilical cords all over again and refreshed."

"I guessed a little of this," Nick said. "Why did they suddenly put you to work on the whole project?"

"They are a little scared. I'm not the only one." She laughed bitterly. "Someone broke into the big building this morning and killed one of their specimens that was programmed as a guard. They don't know if it was a burglar or a spy."

"Industrial spy?"

"That's what they said. But I think they're afraid of the law. And they should be. That man I grafted tissue onto is not dead."

"Well-built redheaded man?"

She gasped. "How did you know?"

"Guy like that is missing."

"Oh." She slumped against him despondently. "That's not all—"

"Tell me. You'll feel better."

"They have Martha Wagner in the lab. I wasn't supposed to see her, but once inside the top security lab it's hard to hide anything. Just a giant room with equipment and the lab tables and stuff."

Nick's neck felt cold. "What are they going to do with her?"

He put the question softly, grinding the edge off the words. "Maybe they'll use her for grafts," Greta replied sadly. "They are devils. Or Rick might try to breed her to one of the synthetics. Of course it wouldn't work, I don't believe. But that's the way his mind goes."

"These guys are leaving themselves wide open," Nick observed. "Should we call in the police?"

"Whatever you think best," Greta answered. "I'm afraid of them. I know the type—"

"From the—old times, you mean?"

"Yes."

"Do both Rick and Benn speak German fluently?"

"Oh yes. We often use it."

Nick rubbed his chin and found it damp. He ran his hand on around his neck. The thin film of damp, cold perspiration went all the way around. He had suggested police to see what she would say. Benn and Rick were fools to keep Hubie and Martha in that lab, unless—

"What do they do with a dead synthetic man?" he asked.

"Acid shred mill," Greta answered dully. "Like a big garbage disposal unit."

"Is it in the top security lab?"

"Yes."

"Do you think—if we brought in the police—they might drop your redheaded specimen and Martha into the shredding mill?"

"Ach!" Greta gripped his hand. "That is why they are both in that end of the room. Of course. Uhhh—" She finished with a sound of sad disgust.

"I saw a lot of activity around your building when I went by on the trucks today," Nick observed. "I wonder what they're up to. There are eleven trailers spotted at the dock, including the one I brought up. Most I've ever seen there. Now that I know they don't have any products to ship from that building . . . makes me wonder. Think they're going to transfer those synthetics someplace?"

"I think so. Maybe they are just scared."

"They don't scare. With that shredding mill, they don't have to. Although they're nervous. But when they can get rid of evidence without a trace in a couple of minutes—they hold the whip."

"So why do you say they are nervous? Rick didn't look nervous. He looked murderous."

"I think they killed Pete Wagner. They're wondering if he wrote up his suspicions. They've taken a long chance in grabbing his sister. To check her out with truth serums, I imagine, plus maybe your idea about Rick and his breeding games. They were going to make Pete's death look accidental but their plan went sour."

Greta sighed. "Such madness. I thought I left it forever—"

Nick stroked her arm comfortingly, turned her and kissed her. She melted against him like a frightened child, rather than a well-groomed woman of considerable years—not all of which showed. She murmured in his ear, "I have saved some money. Let's get away from this horror."

"No. We are going to profit by it or I'm going to bust trying. I want you to drive me into the parking lot beside the big building. You know that clump of little spruces near the main entrance at the edge of the lot?"

She gasped. "No! You cannot—"

"I damn well can," he said sternly. "I'm not letting that

bunch get away with murder, if that's in their mind about those two prisoners. And baby—if they've developed something big, I'm telling them that I'm cutting myself in. Of course I mean you and me, but I won't mention you in case I slip up. I'll—"

"No! No!" Greta squalled. "I won't—"

"Okay. I'll get in by myself. The hard way—"

It took him twenty minutes to stop her tears and convince her he meant it. Another twenty to drive to the Alpine and don his dark clothes and equipment; the combat and destruction underbelt this time, the fat one with the C5 and C6 super-plastique and the lethal Big Pierres.

Curled and crouched, sightless in the Porsche, he traced their route by speed and sway. Along the highway, the sharp turn into the gatehouse, past it without a pause as the guards waved on the familiar red car of Doctor Stoltz. A halt at the clump of spruce forty feet from the main entrance of the building. He left the car without a word and heard it depart. He was a dark shape in the center of the short trees, huddled at their base, partially hidden from the powerful floodlights.

At almost the moment Nick convinced Greta to cooperate, Kenny Abbott, Chet Shirtcliff and Bart Auchincloss were admitted to Benn's office, where the big boss and Robert Rick and Pearly Abbott awaited them. Doctors Nimura and von Dirksen left as they entered. Kenny shuddered at the odor from the two scientists. Scent of the trade, he thought. They trooped around the conference table and, at a gesture from Rick, sat down. Benn alone did not join them. He stayed at his desk across the room, a foreboding figure, faceless behind his hospital mask.

Rick said, "We had to call in you gentlemen this evening because our plans are maturing rapidly. Mr. Shirtcliff has been able to assemble pilots and ships to move our initial production of the new line. You remember Chet?"

"Certainly," Kenny answered. It was always good to say something the big brass could not argue with, yet showed you were hep. "He was Pearly's pilot. We replaced him with Jim Perry."

The room was absolutely silent.

Kenny had the uncomfortable feeling that what he said had paralyzed Benn and Rick. The mask of the apparitionlike gargoyle behind the desk angled slightly and fixed on *him*. He squirmed. Rick leaned forward and turned, giving him a look that made Kenny shiver.

"Who?" Rick asked.

"Jim Perry," Kenny repeated. "He came with us as a truckdriver. No complaints there. And he turned out to be a first-class pilot. Excellent flyer. Right, Uncle Pearly?"

Pearly's antennae caught the menace in the air, but he couldn't tell from whence it blew. He replied cautiously, "A fine flyer."

Rick choked, cleared his throat. "One of our truckers? And he flies you too? But he is not on the employee list—"

Kenny thought fast, then brightened. "He's a new man. He'll be on the next one."

A shower of articles flew past Kenny's head. The boss— Mr. Benn—had thrown his desk set at *him!* The left-handed cast had gone high, but Kenny ducked instinctively. A paperweight—a 40 mm. shell welded to a silver base—whizzed at him with better aim. It took skin from his skull, and it hurt. Kenny yelped.

"Hey!" Pearly said, and began to talk meaninglessly in his confusion.

" 'Raus!" Benn yelled, and began to shout a torrent of words in several languages.

Kenny didn't understand the words, but they were plainly curses and expletives. He saw that mysterious hidden hand come into view. Metal! An intricate mechanical limb! And even at this distance he guessed suddenly that a black snout on the contrivance was a gun. Kenny yelped. The gun pointed at him. He tried to jump out of his chair and it fell over sideways and he went down tangled in it.

Blam! The roar filled the room.

On its echo Robert Rick shouted, "Nein!" He jumped up and ran to Benn, talking rapidly in German.

Chet Shirtcliff and Bart Auchincloss beat Kenny and Pearly to the door by ten feet. They got it open and went through, but nephew and uncle hit the aperture at the same instant and wedged there for a moment. Kenny's back crawled as he struggled for freedom, anticipating a bullet. His uncle knocked him backward with a sweep of an arm. The few seconds it took Kenny to get up on his knees and crawl through the door and around the corner felt like a few years. Then he sprang to his feet and ran after the others.

The electrically locked door to the reception area was open. The night guard, from the local group and forbidden to enter the plant himself, was standing at his desk watching Pearly disappear. "What happened?" he yelped as Kenny galloped by him and out into the night.

Rick, the quick thinker, stuck his head out of the office and yelled, "Just an experiment. It exploded. Okay now. Close that gate and stay at your post."

Hidden in the spruce clump, Nick watched a fascinating scene. They came out the main door at top panic speed—first a stranger, then Auchincloss, then Pearly Abbott and finally Kenny. They ran to their cars in the executive lot and departed with roaring engines, squealing rubber and erratic steering.

Nick debated swiftly, expecting pursuers. When none appeared, he decided that whatever the excitement was in there might be helpful. He ran across the lawn and through the double doors. The civilian guard had his back to him, giving the remote-lock gate a test push. It was secure until released by the button at his desk or the handle on the other side.

The guard was felled and secured as swiftly as a man could be. A two-finger jab, no harder than necessary. His own handkerchief thrust in his mouth and secured with his tie. His wrists and ankles tightly bound with nylon ties which Nick whipped from his belt like a cowboy's piggin' strings.

Nick pushed the guard down behind the desk, opened the barrier with the button and a shove from a chair. He stood in the long hall as the door clicked shut behind him. Everything was suddenly very quiet.

He walked soundlessly past an office door, heard voices behind another. He decided against risking discovery—his first interest was that top security lab, which logically might be near the computer-programming room he had located on his first penetration of the building. The one with the man in white at the console.

A barrier door across the corridor halted him for a moment. It was marked in large blue letters: NO ADMITTANCE. AUTHORIZED PERSONNEL ONLY. DANGER. He decided they had at least two grades of passes—blue and red. "I'm cleared for them all," he murmured as he went through the door.

This corridor was one of the all-gleaming-white, all-glazed-facing-tile types he had seen before. It was either the one he had previously entered from the back of the building or the one on the floor below. In the distance he saw figures cross back and forth. One was walking toward him. Nick bolted into a small office. Among garments on a metal wall hanger he found a full-length white smock. He put it on, then from a pocket in his belt he took a white full-head mask and slipped it over his head.

He caught a glimpse of himself in a small wall mirror. Picturesque, he thought, the abominable snowman meets Dracula's children. Because the smock restricted his reach to the belt beneath his shirt, he took out two of the super-Pierres, carrying them inside his palms with their flesh-colored pull-rings over his middle finger.

There was a clipboard, like a hospital patient's chart, on a wall hook. He grabbed it as he stepped back into the hall. Several figures were closer, most in white, some with face masks. He walked briskly toward them and the stairs he had used before.

Like a doctor, preoccupied with the data in his hand—perhaps the details of a complex case or a handicapper's suggestions for the day's races—Nick passed several people. He didn't look up, although two of them turned to look after him questioningly. He stood out like a giant snowman brought to life, and—if they thought about it—his dark trousers weren't regulation.

He went quickly and lightly down the iron stairs and along the racks of silent synthetics. He had to veer around three workers who were using the gantry crane to pack some of the giant culture tubes in a steel shipping case which held six of the units. From the corner of his eye Nick saw one of them carefully disconnecting an umbilical cord.

When he reached the door with the red warnings: DAN-

GER. KEEP OUT. AUTHORIZED STAFF ONLY, he didn't even pause. He opened and closed it in stride. He was inside the console room.

Passing the control console, he nodded to the white-coated director without actually looking at him. He went through another of the doors with the bright red warnings and closed it behind himself and found out he was—nowhere.

This was what "top security" meant. He faced a stainless-steel door with a large metal dial on it, like a safe combination. There were no crevices for explosives, and anyway he would kill himself if he blasted in the tiny chamber.

Nick rarely showed emotion even in a really tight spot, but now he swore, so softly the sound didn't reach floor level. He fiddled with the dial, studied it, felt for clues. Nothing. They didn't make them any more the way they did in Jimmy Valentine's day. He thought about the man at the console. Make him open it? What if he didn't have top clearance and didn't know the combination?

The door through which he had come was pulled open. Nick pretended to be startled, dropped his clipboard, went down on his hands and knees, found it, dropped it again.

"Oh, I'm sorry," said a white-coated man carrying a surgical case. "Let me help you—"

"I'm so nearsighted," Nick mumbled behind his white mask. "And I take my glasses off because they steam up on account of the mask and I'm always leaving them someplace. . . ." He brushed himself off, finished plaintively, "I'm going back to get them."

He went out the door. The man with the surgical case went in—undoubtedly smiling sympathetically, Nick decided. Nick gave him three seconds, then whirled and went into the security chamber again. The man had just opened the inner door. Nick slipped a super-Pierre off one hand, used it for a chop, a two-finger jab; swift, effective, and, if perfectly delivered, unlikely to do permanent harm. The same blows delivered by an amateur can be fatal.

They were in an entrance L or lobby beyond which a large laboratory loomed with a forest of equipment, machinery, long tables and much shining glass and white tile. Nick stepped into the big room.

There were five people at work, or at some devil's game, among the pieces of strange flesh and odd human organs that pulsed in glass tanks and containers. He saw Martha Wagner, nude on a sort of operating table. Then he saw Hubie Dumont and gritted his teeth.

Hubie was on an autopsy table with its top partly covered by a rubber mat. He was alive, but horribly distorted and carved up. His body and head looked bloated, and Nick guessed that what he viewed weighed 300 pounds. Hubie's chest and abdominal cavities had been opened, by the looks of the sutures and biobandages, and tubes ran from him in several places. There were patches of blood under him, looking purple against the mat, and across his eyes had been taped a bandage. Someone of those who had worked on him must have been squeamish.

In Nick's imagination the torn meat on the table seemed to change as he watched, like a fade-in fade-out film. He saw Hubie as he had known him—healthy, young, proud of his strength and eager for life. Then the picture swelled into the monstrosity that was there. Nick wondered—can you put Humpty Dumpty together again? He realized that if he were this Humpty Dumpty—he wouldn't want them to try.

He turned and walked slowly into the big lab, pretending to study his clipboard.

Marvin Benn's exasperation and vehemence were fiery but short-lived. "On the payroll!" he roared at Rick. "On the damn payroll! Why didn't you *find him*, Heinrich? Now do you see who killed Felix? Ah haa! Because Perry was the man in Dumont's room. And he's the one who got in here yesterday and killed Pfiek 287. Just when we had him programmed right and living longer too—"

Rick wasn't especially disturbed. He and Benn had been through too much together for even this disaster to arouse real enmity. The facts interested him more, like a man studying a dangerous puzzle. "Better not use my old name, Marvin. Someday somebody might hear it. Of course young Abbott is a fool. But I see how the time lag hid Perry's name from us on the employee list."

"Hah," Benn snorted. He sagged back in his chair,

shrugged, and methodically began to reload the empty chamber in the gun built into his artificial hand. "But he wormed his way into Pearly's confidence. 'A fine flyer,' he said. I wish they had crashed—*kaput*. And how much has he found out around here? Imagine—driving our own trucks!"

"Not much," Rick rubbed his chin slowly, as stolid now as a member of the general staff contemplating a flanking movement by an army while the center feinted (his uncle had once ordered such a move and lost 175,000 men; but since the British and French lost an equal number plus 200 yards of ground, Uncle was decorated for it). "Our security up to now has been unbreachable. Where do you think he is from, Marvin? Interpol, AXE, CIA, FBI, the British? Or perhaps our competitors—Capallaro's Sicilians? The Greek Boatman? Or even that London crowd which is getting more and more ingenious—and dangerous."

"I don't know," Benn replied. "But if he's the one from AXE who has cost us so much—I'm almost ready to die with him to get him."

"Don't count me in on that without a consultation." It was Rick's version of nonchalant humor.

"I said *almost* ready." Benn picked up the telephone, consulted an address book, dialed. "Hello—hello—Duke?"

He listened, nodded, then spoke slowly. "This is your friend whom you have not seen. The one the envelope comes from. You recognize the voice?" Pause. "Ah, good. You have a new driver. Jim Perry. He is a police spy." Benn held the phone away from his ear. Rick could hear the squawking tones, like the chatter of an insane mechanical doll.

"Easy, easy," Benn shut off the flow of words. "You could not help it. But if you should have a chance to—divert him, let's say, divert him so that he will never trouble us again—the envelopes will contain ten times as much—for ten years."

When Benn hung up Rick nodded admiringly. "Your man on the dock?"

"Yes. The old spy system is the best. Lots of people and regular payments—if you have the money. That was Rainey. He couldn't help it if he didn't suspect Perry. But if he shows up tomorrow—we have him."

The intercom buzzed. Benn looked surprised, answered.

A heavy voice filled the room. "Mr. Benn. We've captured a man in the top security lab. The Wagner girl let slip his name. Jim. Big fellow. Masked when we got him. Dark tan. Brown hair."

CHAPTER IX

Duke Rainey hung up the phone with a crash after his talk with Benn. He ran out of the house without a word to his wife and swore monotonously as he raced to the plant, hitting 85 on the stretch to the gatehouse. He parked beside the tractor assigned to "Jim Perry" for a morning run, and whipped it through the grounds to the docks at the big building.

He was surprised by the activity at this time of night. Men were loading big metal shipping containers into some of the trailers, but the one Perry would pick up—4107—stood silent and empty.

Rainey coupled up, hauled it to the dock at the other loading platforms a quarter-mile away and parked it near the shop. He fussed with the sanders, and then filled each one with ten quarts of S.A.E. 40 oil. He removed an air hose and replaced it with one of his own creation, one with an odd triple valve fitted in it. Then he drove the trailer back to its position and reparked the tractor.

Only as he was driving away did he stop cursing. What a narrow squeak! He should have guessed when Perry was so willing to help with a drug deal. He made it sound so damn good. Well, let Perry think about that tomorrow when he tried to brake going down the mountain. The cab gauge would read perfectly, but there'd be no brakes on the trailer. And when he sanded to help the tractor brake's hold, the oil under those spinning wheels would finish the job. He hoped Perry jackknifed off Burro Bend. Four hundred feet straight down.

"Jim Perry" had other worries at the moment. He had

146

moved through the big lab, trying to look busy, searching for
a plan to get Martha and Hubie out of this squirrel house. As
he stood watching Martha he saw her eyelids flicker. She was
either coming out of the drugs they had used on her or she
was faking. One of the white-coats came up and felt her
pulse. Nick stood motionless like a doctor on consultation.

White-coat said through his face mask, "She oughtta be
coming out of it. Maybe I'd better give her another shot—"

Nick shook his head, *negative,* slowly and authoritatively.
White-coat glanced at him again, lifted one shoulder and
turned away.

They got him after he had made his second circle of the
room. Four of them came around the corner like AFL end
men on a good day. He didn't have a chance, and he had
never seen or felt anything like it.

Battling *one* perfectly programmed synthetic man had almost been a draw—against four you needed room and a
small slice of time. They hit him as he half turned, diving
aside. He never hit the floor. There was one on his left arm
and one on his right, one picking him up from in front and
the other circling neatly to apply a back strangle. The ones
on his arms applied the double armlocks with his elbows levered over their bent forearms. They could break even his
powerful arms like a man snapping kindling.

When he was pinned, motionless, helpless, they stopped,
holding him upright. From around the corner strolled the
man he had disabled near the door. He was holding a wet
cloth on his neck. He looked at Nick, hard green eyes above
a gauze panel. "Hello, friend. I owe you something. Who are
you?"

"I'm from *Life* magazine," Nick answered. "We smell a
story."

"Think of the alternative," the man said. He walked to the
table on which Martha lay, and called, "Bring him over here.
Take that mask off."

Nick didn't touch the ground as they carried him across
the floor. The synthetic behind him lifted off his hood mask.

Other white-coated men were gathering around, like in-
terns in an operating room. The man holding the compress
on his neck said, "You're a stranger to me. Any of you know

him?" When no one answered he said, "Ammonia." Someone handed him a vial. He broke it, held it under Martha's nostrils. She gagged, sat up, her eyes rolling.

The synthetics pushed Nick toward the table. Martha's vision focused on him. She said sadly, "Oh—Jim—I'm sorry—"

"Jim," the man said. "Jim who?"

"McNulty," Nick replied.

"I doubt it," the other said dryly. He went to the end of the room and they could hear the murmur of his voice talking at the telephone.

Nick flexed his fingers a little. He could still, perhaps, pull the releases on the super-Pierres. There was nothing else he could do. Every time he lifted a leg an inch all the synthetics stiffened at once. His arms threatened to break, and the one with the strangle was just barely letting him breathe.

But he couldn't use the Pierres. Those amazing little lethal gas bombs, the pride and joy of Stuart, AXE's technical wizard, would kill Martha and Hubie, although probably Hubie would want it that way. The little globes held their deadly charges under astonishingly high PSI, and it dispersed so violently that seconds after release you couldn't see the microparticles. Indeed, their pressure was so great that if you dropped one in a fire the explosion would be the equivalent of four pounds of trinitrotoluene. Their pins were held in by their own back pressure, and only a tiny equalizing valve enabled you to pull them out. A beautiful device. The only weapon he could use—and he couldn't use it.

The man who had gone to the telephone guided Benn and Rick into the room.

The entrance of the master and his cohort was impressive. Six synthetics in dark suits marched behind them and lined up along the wall like a palace guard.

Benn, a rather small, limping figure that walked oddly erect, like a broken mechanical soldier, marched up and faced Nick. "So, Mr. Perry, have you got what you wanted? Eh? Because death is what you've got. In one minute. I wanted to see your face. The face of a man who has cost me millions." He turned to Rick. "Would you say he's the one? From the pictures taken in Jakarta?"

Rick peered at Nick from several angles, then shrugged.

"He could be. Same size and skull. Different hair, but they change that. Anyway—eliminate him, I suggest."

"We will—we will." Benn's voice rose, just a little, as it came through the mask. There was a wet spot widening around the mouth that fascinated Nick because it was irregular. "You're the one," Benn said emphatically. "You got my own allies, the Chinese, to sink my Portugee ketch. The finest ship I ever had. A man doesn't get over that."

He paused, and Nick said, "I never heard of you before. What's a Portugee ketch?"

"Liar. You went to Dumont's room in Forge. Are you two with the same organization?"

"I don't know any Dumont."

"Oh—then you won't mind. Pfiek 391. The shred mill. Four four eight. The man on table fourteen—"

He snapped the words like a drillmaster and the synthetics moved like a double-time close-order team. One lifted the cover from a four-foot trap near the wall, touched a switch. The oily substance in the well-like opening stirred, boiled, smoked a little. Another appeared carrying Hubie in a plastic blanket.

Benn pointed. "In there."

Hubie—or Hubie's cadaver—was eased over the edge into the dark roily pool and simply vanished. There was a brief grinding sound, as if a meatchopper was working underwater, and then nothing. The liquid continued to percolate.

"And you're next," Benn said to Nick. "I'd like to take a lot of time with you, but I don't know how much damage you've done already. And you can be dangerous. I've studied your tricks."

"Okay, *mein herren*," Nick said. "But what about the girl? She has nothing to do with us."

Nick felt that Benn smiled behind the mask. "Ah, yes. But she called you Jim. Well—I never was one to waste good female flesh. Pfiek 528—take the woman to my plane. You are responsible for her."

Benn stepped back away from the deadly opening in the floor. He couldn't resist letting Nick watch one of the synthetics hurry from his post along the wall, whip a plastic sheet around Martha and carry her out over his shoulder like a bundle of rugs. "Wait for us," Benn snapped.

Nick said, "What are you going to do with these synthetics? I don't see any payoff. Are you completely nuts?"

Benn came closer to him. "Crazy? Me? Sometimes I wonder. Don't we all? Don't worry about the payoff, as you call it. It will be the greatest the world has ever seen. I may even rebuild an empire. Think—in an age of violence the haves are so deathly afraid of violence they scream for more instruments of it. More arms—more police—kill the violent!" His voice rose; then he brought it down to a coo. "How easily they will cower before my emotionlessly violent men, eh? Pay or die. Do as I say or die! Your rulers and your financial kings will fight for places in line to kiss my boots! Here, they'll scream, take! Leave me a little and kill them, not me!"

"Not all," Nick said, but the words caught in his throat.

"Yes, all!" Benn yelled. "Because I promise them law and order, too!"

From the doorway where the synthetic stood holding Martha sounded a scream. It was high powered, a spine-ripping, nerve-shaking caterwaul. A howl of fear and anger that filled the chamber and echoed from the hard walls, a metallic crash of sound from a throat that had practiced shouting orders above the clatter of a room packed with noisy diners. Benn hopped toward the door where the synthetic held Martha. Rick followed him. Martha cut loose with a second crescendo. Benn called over his shoulder to the synthetics, "Dump him in."

Nick curled his fingers over his palms, held his breath and levered the pins out of the super-Pierres. He was carried toward the acid shredmill. One step, two—then the creature on his left let go his grip. The one in front of him fell. Nick wrenched free of the synthetic on his right as he staggered, reaching for his throat, and toppled away.

Nick leaped for the L and the doorway, Wilhelmina appearing in his hand as if tossed there, although he had to lift the smock to make the draw. He shot the synthetic holding Martha as he was turning toward the door, one-two-three slugs before he went down. Benn and Rick vanished around the tile wall. Nick dropped Wilhelmina to catch Martha as she fell, whipped up a hand to cover her nose and mouth in a vicious hold as if determined to strangle her. She writhed, kicked and clawed at him as he dragged her to the door with the combination lock which was swinging shut behind Benn and Rick. He got her through, wishing he had made studies on just how fast super-Pierres spread their deadly load. He didn't stop moving until they were through the console room and had another door closed behind them.

The white-coated man at the control unit stood up, yelled, "What in hell's going on in here?" And fell like an uprooted pole as the door swung shut and hid him from Nick's sight.

Nick was well scarred when he finally released his grip on Martha's nose and mouth. She gasped for air as he patted her on the back and rubbed her neck. She required thirty seconds of gulping air before she said, "You bastard; you tried to strangle me," and then burst into tears.

"Deadly gas," he said into her ear. "Can you walk?"

She stood up promptly, tried to draw the plastic sheet around her nakedness, realized it was transparent and cast it aside. Nick took off his smock and gave it to her. He peeked out into the corridor. Benn and Rick had vanished. He said, "Wait here. I want my gun."

Holding his breath again, just in case, he ran back through the console room. The body of a synthetic, jammed in the door with the safe combination, held it open. The lab room was as silent as a grave—and a grave it was for the figures sprawled here and there in the flat, boneless crumples of the dead. He found Wilhelmina and ran back to Martha. He was just in time. Marching toward them past the big culture racks came a dozen synthetics. The loading gang had vanished, the gantry crane chains were still swinging. When the synthetics saw him they broke left and right, coming along the sides of the passage like a well-drilled infantry squad. Nick pulled Martha toward the nearest iron stairway. "Up—as fast as you can."

Martha was fast. She leaped up the coarse iron treads three at a time, bare feet or not. They were halfway up when the synthetics rushed, pounding down the room with astonishing speed. Nick climbed and let them come, then turned and used the remaining slugs in Wilhelmina to topple the first three back down onto the others. It was rapid fire, a thunder volley of sound—but every bullet was aimed for a skull, not just for a head but for a pinpoint on the head. He had burned a lot of powder to practice for deadly dangerous moments like this. He didn't regret an ounce of it. You wouldn't stop these creatures with flesh wounds or Spanish shooting.

He guided Martha along one of the white corridors, tore open a door which led out to the loading docks. There was no advantage in trying to reach the front of the building and meeting another tribe of purposeful artificial soldiers. As they left the stairway he saw the synthetics rushing up the gangway. They didn't scare, either.

The fresh air smelled grand. "Run," he yelled at Martha, and turned and tossed a blast grenade at an angle across the corridor in the direction they had come. Then, holding the door wedged open with a foot, he threw a shower of Stuart's best items at the same point, hoping some would ricochet off the tile and find their way down the stair opening.

Blast grenades—two. Splinter grenades that shed a hundred razorlike particles—three. C6 bombs with fifteen-second timers—two. He felt like a Christmas tree plucking itself clean of explosive gifts.

The first blast grenade went off as he released the door and ran after Martha. In the direction she had taken, toward the end of the long dock, a truck's engine was roaring. He heard Martha's scream and then a shot. He caught up with her cowering behind a trailer. "It's Rick," she gasped. "In that truck. He shot at me."

Two workers crawled out from under the platform as explosions continued to boom inside the plant. "Hey—what's happened?"

"Explosion in the lab," Nick said. "Go see if you can help 'em."

The men went down the dock. Nick led Martha in the other direction. As the truck and trailer circled under the floodlights he caught the number on the back of the big aluminum body—4107.

He said, "I've got to get a car—"

The whole world moved sideways, removing their footing for an instant and knocking them flat. He tried to cushion

Martha's fall, but they were tumbled like children's toy soldiers hit by a ball.

The doors leading to the docks spewed fire and debris from the interior of the building as if they were shotgun mouths. Glass and parts of doors hit the hillside three hundred feet away. The sound pushed in on their eardrums. It sounded as if an A-bomb had gone off inside the Reed-Farben main building. When Nick could swallow, he dragged Martha away from the flames which spewed from every opening in the structure.

"Are you cut?" he asked.

"No," she answered.

"If that place had windows in it we'd have been sliced like cheese."

"Did you—plant a bomb?"

"You couldn't carry a bomb in your pocket strong enough to do that. I think my grenades must have reached the oxygen and other stuff."

A secondary explosion shook the earth as they climbed the hill. Nick said, "We might as well walk around to the highway. There won't be anything left of the cars in the lot."

"They took mine to one of the hangars at the airport. I heard them say so."

"We'll probably find Hubie's there, too. How'd they get you?"

"Just stopped me on the road. They said I had to know more than I told them."

Nick squeezed her hand. "You did, didn't you?"

"Yes. And I didn't tell *them*, either."

Nick went down the next day to inspect the wreckage of the tractor and trailer 4107. No bodies, no blood. It was frustrating. As he was detaching a strange valve and airhose, a gray-haired man clambered briskly down the embankment. It was David Hawk. After they had exchanged greetings Hawk said, "You were so fascinating on the phone I thought I'd better get over here."

"Glad you did." Nick waved the coupling in a grease-smeared fist. "This may tell us something. Funny valve for an airhose line."

They climbed up the grade. Hawk said, "Very nice work, Nick. McGee and a team are at Reed-Farben checking loose ends. They'll need you when you have time to write up the C report."

"I'll go down there now."

"Good. If you wrap it up you can leave for Washington tomorrow. I know you've got a lot of accumulated time off coming. . . ."

"Mind if I stay here for a day or two?" Nick looked up at the towering mountains. "Nice country to take a few deep breaths in."

"With company? Like Martha? Or Greta?"

"They deserve a little relaxation. Any charges on Greta?"

"Probably not. She told you as soon as she observed a felony. It would be a weak out in court, but we aren't looking to cause people trouble. Especially lovely ladies who have been through plenty."

Nick stayed in the mountains for over a week. On the first evening he drove Martha up to the ledge with the view, and discovered that it had been genuine, that first night.

Something unusual and rare, as he had decided before. Worth preserving . . . and repeating.

THE RED RAYS   A423-60¢
A bizarre new sex ray is being used by the Red
Chinese to launch a global death game.

PEKING/THE TULIP AFFAIR   A424-60¢
Two exciting adventures under one cover—danger
stalks Killmaster from Germany to Peking's Imperial
Palace.

BERLIN   A455-60¢
Two agents have already been killed and Nick is the
only one who can stop the rise of a new Hitler!

THE HUMAN TIME BOMB   A456-60¢
Killmaster is faced by a master army of men and
women—who are neither dead or alive!

DANGER KEY   A491-60¢
Mr. Judas returns to settle an old score with
Killmaster.

THE COBRA KILL   A495-60¢
Nick Carter and a beautiful nymphomaniac team up
on a wild manhunt in Malaysia.

THE LIVING DEATH   A496-60¢
A hideous destruction-machine is stealing the minds
of the world's most brilliant scientists.

OPERATION CHE GUEVARA   A509-60¢
A dead guerrilla leader kept strangely alive and a
secret kept by two beautiful, treacherous women!

THE DOOMSDAY FORMULA   A520-60¢
When the Japanese Communists threaten to sink
Hawaii to the bottom of the sea, the call goes out
for Nick Carter.

OPERATION SNAKE   A559-60¢
A nightmare mission that pits Nick Carter against a
power-mad monk in a horrifying global tug-of-war.

THE CASBAH KILLERS   A560-60¢
A macabre manhunt for a missing agent.

THE CHINA DOLL   A638-60¢
Nick Carter is the first white man in the "Forbidden City" of Peking.

CHECKMATE IN RIO   A639-60¢
Sex and savagery are the facts of life for every agent.

ISTANBUL   A640-60¢
America's super-spy finds sultry love and sudden violence in the Middle East.

THE WEAPON OF NIGHT   A641-60¢
Total annihilation threatens under cover of paralyzing power failures.

A complete list of Nick Carter novels can be found on page 2 of this book. All books are 60¢ each. Just fill in the book number on the coupon and send in with your remittance.